∽

Love Unleashed

Sit, Stay, Love

Fetching Sweetness

∽

Fetching Sweetness

DANA MENTINK

HARVEST HOUSE PUBLISHERS
EUGENE, OREGON

Scripture quotations are taken from

The Holy Bible, New International Version®, NIV®. Copyright © 1973, 1978, 1984, 2011 by Biblica, Inc.® Used by permission. All rights reserved worldwide.

The New King James Version®. Copyright © 1982 by Thomas Nelson, Inc. Used by permission. All rights reserved.

The King James Version of the Bible.

Cover by Left Coast Design

Cover photo © Jess Wealleans / Shutterstock

The author is represented by MacGregor Literary, Inc.

FETCHING SWEETNESS
Copyright © 2016 by Dana Mentink
Published by Harvest House Publishers
Eugene, Oregon 97402
www.harvesthousepublishers.com

ISBN 978-0-7369-6623-8 (pbk.)
ISBN 978-0-7369-6624-5 (eBook)

Library of Congress Cataloging-in-Publication Data
    Names: Mentink, Dana, author.
    Title: Fetching sweetness / Dana Mentink.
    Description: Eugene Oregon : Harvest House Publishers, [2016]
    Identifiers: LCCN 2016002899 (print) | LCCN 2016006937 (ebook) | ISBN
        9780736966238 (softcover) | ISBN 9780736966245 ()
    Subjects: LCSH: Man-woman relationships--Fiction. | GSAFD: Romantic suspense
        fiction. | Christian fiction. | Love stories.
    Classification: LCC PS3613.E496 F48 2016 (print) | LCC PS3613.E496 (ebook) |
        DDC 813/.6--dc23
    LC record available at http://lccn.loc.gov/2016002899

Printed in the United States of America

16 17 18 19 20 21 22 23 24 / BP-GL / 10 9 8 7 6 5 4 3 2 1

Heaven goes by favor. If it went by merit, you would stay out and your dog would go in.

MARK TWAIN

⚮

"For I know the plans I have for you," declares the LORD, "plans to prosper you and not to harm you, plans to give you hope and a future."

JEREMIAH 29:11

One

Stephanie regretted driving over the wedding cake. She'd had hours of bus travel during the last leg of her endless journey from New York to mull over her actions when her seatmate, Mrs. Granato, had dozed off. Regret bit at her with needle-sharp teeth. It had been a lovely cake, white with strawberry filling, frilly little rosettes, and the odd string of pearls which were somehow edible. The cake was certainly not deserving of being flattened. And reversed over. The memory made her cringe. Who would imagine Stephanie Pink indulging in a moment of madness? Plenty of people, she thought ruefully.

As the bus wheezed to a stop, she straightened her aching shoulders, stowed her regret in the under-seat compartment, and listened to the driver who announced, "Big Thumb."

Mrs. Granato awoke with a yawn in the seat next to her, smiled, and patted her bunker of hair into place. "I'll be praying for you, Stephanie. No more running over desserts or anything else, right? God's got a better plan for you."

"Yes, ma'am." Stephanie felt her cheeks grow warm. She'd shared too much in the four-hour ride, but Mrs. Granato was such a good listener. Compassion seemed to ooze out of her, extracting all of Stephanie's secrets. She was like a Christian Svengali.

"Here, love." Mrs. Granato pressed a miniature book in Stephanie's hand. "Read it when you can, since you didn't bring your Bible. And drink lots of water. It's hot here."

At least the woman wasn't foisting a manuscript on her. Nope. Mrs. Granato was one of the few people in the known universe who did not seem to be writing a book. This volume she'd been handed, smaller than her cell phone, was entitled *Divine Promises*. She no doubt felt it would be of help to someone with Stephanie's destructive tendencies. Mrs. Granato was a glass-half-full kind of gal.

Stephanie thanked her and peered through the bus windows, excitement building. This had to be the place. What other town could possibly be better for an assignation to hand over a priceless package? She couldn't have written a finer scene in a novel. Tiny, brick-fronted buildings lined the streets and the smell of hay and diesel fuel drifted in through the open bus door. One man in overalls—real overalls, yet—sat on a bench in the shade of a gnarled tree, reading a newspaper. Imagine that. A *newspaper*. She'd thought they'd gone the way of the dodo. Scanning the street, she looked for her quarry, her stomach tightening into delicious prickles. So close.

Her cell phone informed her it was a few minutes before nine. If she believed in that sort of thing, she'd have chalked her timely arrival up to a miracle. Two endless flights and a miserable delay due to some mechanical mischief in Phoenix. Then deplaning in what passed for a municipal airport in Redding, where she'd caught a bus. Bumping along in this big metal sarcophagus for hours, she had actually managed to arrive on time, if somewhat rumpled. The travel pains would be forgotten, every dusty mile of them, as soon as she bagged her quarry.

She said one more goodbye to Mrs. Granato, who kissed her

on the cheek and looked into her eyes. An odd clog formed in Stephanie's throat. Travel-induced emotional meltdown? Had to be. *Business at hand, Pink.* She unkinked her five-foot-three frame and marched down the steps. The bus rumbled away, leaving her in a cloud of exhaust and triumph. Stephanie Pink, literary agent's assistant, had arrived. Flush with confidence that she was about to cross a threshold she'd waited for all her life, she mechanically reached for the journal in her suitcase to jot a quick note.

Words formed in her head. *I'm here, Ian. We're here.*

Fingers twitching, she whirled around. Her suitcase, the pink one with the matching luggage tags, was not there. She'd left it on the bus that had just rattled out of town. She stood dumbly as this information sank in. Three deep breaths. The old Stephanie, the one who drove over wedding cakes, would have pitched an ugly fit, but not now, not with her destiny waiting. The new Stephanie Pink was not even flustered...much.

"I'll be on a plane home in a couple of hours anyway," she muttered to no one.

She scanned for the café, the only eating establishment in the town of Big Thumb, California, south of Redding and north of nowhere. There it was, tucked under the shade of a cottonwood tree across the street from a gas station with one pump and a post office with an attached bait shop.

She scurried across the road, trying to pat into place the ponytail that had lost its chic some sixteen hours prior. *Where are you, Mrs. Wharton?*

The last time she'd seen Agnes Wharton had been thirteen years before, when she'd appeared at a bookstore event in Manhattan that Stephanie and her twin brother, Ian, had skipped their seventh-grade algebra class to attend. Back then, Wharton had been a twitchy, middle-aged woman with her hair plaited into a braid that left frizzy tendrils around the temples. She was in no way the literary giant they'd expected, but Stephanie had subsequently learned that authors were seldom what one expected. Back then, the group had drilled Agnes Wharton with the one question on everyone's mind. When?

When would the precious sequel to *Sea Comes Knocking*, the memoir that had become an instant classic, be delivered? *When?*

The answer is today, Stephanie thought with a thrill of victory.

Today, Stephanie Pink would take possession of the novel that the hungry world had been waiting for, fifteen long years after the first installment. So what if Agnes had become a recluse, without so much as a cell phone? It was charming, in a way, that they'd corresponded exclusively by letter to arrange the meeting in this wee town that had some sort of sentimental meaning for Agnes. Rumors abounded that the eccentric author had not left her remote off-the-grid property in the wilds of Washington since that book signing thirteen years ago in Manhattan, but Stephanie did not believe it. Nor did she care. She would get that manuscript if she had to crawl across the country on her hands and knees, and she would finally see her name neatly lettered on the frosted glass office door. She'd measured one morning in between coffee runs. Klein, Gregory, and Pink Literary Agency. It would just fit. Good thing her last name only had four letters. Pinkerton would never do.

How her brother would have crowed. *I'm close enough to taste it, Ian.*

She shouldered her purse more securely and marched into the Thumb's Corner Café. A quick scan of the tables netted no solitary, literary types.

"Hello," she said to the teen boy behind the counter. "I'm supposed to meet someone here. Her name is Agnes Wharton."

"Haven't had anyone but regulars today 'cept one woman with a braid."

Her breath hitched. "That's her. Where is she?"

"I don't know. She came in and asked for a bowl of water about ten minutes ago and then left. Hasn't been back."

"Great, thanks..." Stephanie suddenly stopped. "A bowl of water? For what?"

He shrugged. She was already pushing back outside. "Never mind. Thank you."

The July sunlight in this rugged part of the world dazzled her eyes. She slipped off her silk blazer, beginning to wish she'd worn a skirt instead of her dress slacks. At least her pumps were low heeled.

Bowl of water? Stephanie sped along the sidewalk toward the only vehicle she saw, an old Chevy Suburban parked one block down, with the passenger door open.

Stephanie stopped alongside it when she noticed the overturned bowl and the stain of spilled water drying rapidly on the sidewalk. There was no one in the car. On the floor of the front passenger seat was a bag with a loaf of bread sticking out of the top. The front seat was crammed with plastic bags stuffed with recently purchased batteries, bags of flour, toothpaste and dental floss, a carton of copier paper, and three scattered white rose petals. The backseat had a blanket spread over it and an old cardboard box on the floor, the perfect size to hold a neatly typed manuscript.

Delicious tension spiraled through her body. "You don't suppose..." she whispered, reaching for the cardboard box. Was she inches away from the sequel to *Sea Comes Knocking*? Her fingers went icy.

She was startled when a woman ran out of the clustered trees. A silvered braid, intense brown eyes. Agnes Wharton. It could be no one else.

Stephanie beamed, feeling like a starstruck teen. "Ms. Wharton, I'm Stephanie Pink from the Klein and Gregory Agency. I'm so..."

The woman ran past her, slammed the passenger car door, and raced to the driver's side.

"Ms. Wharton," Stephanie called. "I'm—" She was about to launch into her introduction for the second time, but Wharton leaped into the driver's seat and gunned the engine.

"Wait," Stephanie said, waving her arms. "I'm here to meet with you. You can't just drive off."

Wharton jammed the car into gear.

The old Stephanie, the one who drove over wedding cakes, sprang in front of the car and whacked her palms on the hot metal of the hood.

"Stop!" she yelled. "I'm trying to talk to you."

Wharton jerked as if she hadn't before noticed the sweating, well-dressed woman sprawled on the hood of her Suburban.

She honked the horn, which made Stephanie jump.

"Get in, or I'll run you over."

Stephanie thought it over for millisecond. Agnes Wharton was clearly nuts. Then again, all writers were a little nuts, and this particular nut held the keys to Stephanie's future. One second ticked by. Two. Hauling open the door, Stephanie hurtled onto the passenger seat.

∽

Rhett Hastings opened one eye and rubbed the shoulder he'd bruised trying to force the trailer door closed that morning. It had been a Herculean effort to park the 1953 Lighthouse Travel Trailer in the first open space he saw at the Big Thumb Campground. He hadn't even hooked the behemoth up to electrical or water. He'd simply unhitched his truck and crawled into the trailer. Sprawled on the musty living room sofa, he'd mumbled an awkward prayer that he was doing what God commanded and not simply making the most colossal mistake of his life, and then he'd fallen asleep until nearly dinnertime on Tuesday.

When he finally swam his way fully into consciousness, he sat up. The sunlight that had streamed in through the window all day left the trailer oven temperature. Sweat dampened his brown hair into those curls that annoyed him. He reached for his phone to text the guy who would come and give him a two-hundred-dollar haircut. Then he remembered. *You don't live that life anymore, Rhett.*

Right. Shoving his fingers through his hair did not improve his look, nor did the stubble of beard on his unshaven chin. He felt the thrill of something again in his stomach, and he wasn't sure if it was fear or exhilaration. Didn't matter. He was way past the penny or pound stage. God had directed him to this hulk of a trailer, which was the symbol of the way forward, the rusting, unwieldy bridge to a new life for Karen. Unless He hadn't, and it wasn't, and Rhett was delusional. It was a possibility.

The trailer needed major renovations. The thing had already been on the rickety side two decades ago when he and his sister had lived in it. The paneling was water damaged, and he had a feeling the entire ceiling in the upper level bedrooms needed to be replaced. As he paced a few steps and tried to get the kinks out of his six-foot-three frame, he noticed a soft spot in the hallway between the living room and the kitchen near the bathroom.

In days gone by, Rhett had been tolerable at helping his Uncle Mel fix up the old trailer, but replacing a ceiling and floor might take some research. He didn't stew about it. A couple of YouTube videos, and he was sure he'd be up to speed on the how-to. He rummaged through the kitchen cupboards until he found the meager supplies he'd purchased the day before. Dried Turkish apricots and Marcona almonds would have to do until he got the power up and running— if he even bothered. One day to get the tire replaced and the door fixed, he figured, and then back on the road. He had a deadline, after all. Schedule, deadline, plan. The words soothed him.

Something flashed by the window, a blur of white. He opened the door to investigate, but he saw nothing except for a thick forest of shrubs. A squirrel chattered from an old tree stump. He chewed a couple of apricots. Now that he was fully alert, he saw he'd managed to select a pretty isolated camping spot. Down to the left, a trickle of water, which was probably closer to a river in the winter, burbled weakly. The ground was covered by pine needles, and the little camp store and pool were so far away he could not even hear the chatter of summer visitors getting in that last swim of the day. If there were any visitors. Big Thumb was not exactly a tourist mecca. He wouldn't have stopped either if he wasn't exhausted, emotionally and physically.

He heard his Uncle Mel repeat in that quiet way of his. "Rhett, you sure about this?"

"No," he'd said, "but I think God is." Uncle Mel probably thought he'd lost his mind. At odd moments, Rhett feared that his uncle was right.

The sound of a car engine caught his attention. Someone was completely ignoring the five-mile-per-hour campground speed limit. He stepped out on the metal porch of the trailer, which groaned under his weight. A Suburban pelted into view, coming to such a sudden stop that it skidded for a few feet on the pine needle carpet.

Two women got out, one older, braid flapping; the other younger, too well dressed for camping or Big Thumb in general. To his utter astonishment, they both raced into the thicket of bushes, leaving the car doors flung open.

He waited a moment to be sure they weren't dealing with nature's call or some such thing, but when he heard them hollering something he couldn't make out, he hopped off the step and headed toward the thicket. He reached it just as the younger girl emerged, her chic twist of dark hair mussed and a rip in the knee of her pants, panic written on her face.

"What's—" he started.

Her dark eyes were wild. "Big dog. White."

"How—"

"Find him!" she shrieked.

Rhett was a man who rarely took orders from anyone, a tendency noted on multiple occasions in his school records. This time, the escalating hysteria in her voice caused him to comply, more out of curiosity than altruism. Something about the frantic woman intrigued him. Pushing through the branches, he searched.

"Hey, doggie. Come on out here, fella."

A half hour later, hot and sweating, he caught sight of the older lady marching grimly back to the Suburban. He followed. The young woman was there now too, looking even more worse for wear than he'd noted before.

"Ms. Wharton," the young woman said in a soothing tone. "Please try to calm down. I'll call the police and animal control. We'll find your dog. I promise. He can't have gotten far."

Ms. Wharton did not appear assuaged. Rhett saw now that she was thin, very thin. Her brown face was webbed with lines and speckled with spots of sun damage.

"I'm sorry," the young woman continued. "We'll fix this, but can we conclude our business first?" She offered a smile, which Rhett had to admit lit her face like a beacon. Dark hair, dark eyes, porcelain skin.

"Your manuscript is priceless," she said. "It would be a tragedy if something happened to it."

Priceless? Now he was hooked.

Ms. Wharton considered for a moment, her mouth working as if she was reciting a speech to herself. Then she stalked to the backseat and hauled out a cardboard box tied with a string, her hands clutched around it so firmly that her knuckles turned white.

The younger woman's eyes danced. "That's it?" she breathed. "I can't believe it. Finally." She held out her hands, fingers trembling slightly.

Ms. Wharton pulled the box tight to her chest. Her voice sounded low and rusty from disuse. "If you want this, you are going to find my dog and bring him to me."

"What?" the woman said, her face turning from ecstasy to puzzlement. "Are you saying you won't give it to me now?"

"Nail on the head, sweetie."

"But Ms. Wharton—"

She freed a hand to point one long bony finger straight at the young woman's chest. "No dog, no manuscript. I'm going home. I hate it here." She shot a look at Rhett. "Too many people now."

"Wait," she cried as Ms. Wharton put the box back into the car and gunned the engine. "You can't just drive off. How will I—"

"Find Sweetness!" Wharton shrieked. Through the open window, Rhett saw the spark of tears in her eyes. Dust swirled from under the churning tires, and then she was gone.

It was like a moment straight out of a classic movie. The young woman's mouth was open as she stared after the departing car, one hand frozen in the air.

"What just happened?" she whispered.

"Seems like she wants you to find her dog," he said, helpfully.

Slowly, very slowly, her gaze swiveled to him. "I feel like screaming."

He stood aside and held the trailer door open. "You can scream in here if you like."

Her eyes narrowed slightly. "And what are you going to do during the screaming?"

He was already pulling on a baseball cap to contain his irritating curls and walking down the road. "Find the dog," he called.

Two

Stephanie's head spun as she stood there between the rusty trailer and the rapidly departing man. The screaming fit was tempting. She'd just been within arm's reach of the manuscript that would change everything, only to have it whisked away. And now she was...where exactly?

She did a slow circle, ignoring the pinch from her pumps. Trees and shrubs surrounded the place, some sort of camp, she'd discerned. Camp. She'd never been to one, but she'd heard camps were places rank with nature where people intentionally banished themselves. In the distance she could make out the blue nylon of a tent and another trailer up at the top of the hill. The quiet was eerie. No bustle of people, no constant stream of city traffic, no smell of the urban life.

In New York City there was never a still time, a silent hour where one could hear everything from falling leaves to the hammering of one's own heart. Where were the honking taxis, the incessant hum of traffic? It made her uneasy, all of this lousy quiet.

"You can salvage this, Stephanie," she said. Swallowing hard, she forced her lungs to carry on working. "Everything will be peachy when you find the dog." Or maybe the man would. He looked hearty and hale, approachable. What dog wouldn't come bounding out of the woods to meet him? He probably had dogs lining up to join him in this camping business. She would just send a quick, vague text to Mr. Klein and tell him there'd been a teeny delay, but the matter was well on its way to a happy resolution.

Panic rippled through her insides. Her purse and cell phone happened to be in the front seat of Agnes Wharton's car. Her palms went clammy. No phone. No money. Not so much as a tissue or a tube of lipstick. Now she did let out a shriek, only one, but it was loud enough to startle two scrub jays from their perch in the trees.

The man reappeared at a run. "What happened?"

"Just a scream," she said, through clenched teeth. "A small one."

"I thought you were going to do that in the trailer."

Stephanie threw up her chin. "This is America. I can scream wherever I like, can't I?"

His brown eyes widened and he broke into a full-lipped smile, brushing pine needles off of his sleeves. "Depends on what you're screaming. You're not allowed to yell 'Fire!' in a theater."

He looked familiar. She tried to place the brown curls that peeked out from under the brim of his baseball cap, the heavy lashes completely wasted on a man, the wide shoulders and muscular forearms showing where he'd rolled up his sleeves. Had she seen him somewhere before? Her stomach tightened. Like on TV's *Ten Most Wanted* or something? What better place for a serial killer to hang out than in Big Thumb. *Don't get crazy, Steph.* "Did you find the dog?"

"No, but I have an idea where he's gone."

Was he a dog whisperer? She felt a spark of hope. "Where?"

"Hot-dog roast today. Can't you smell it?"

Her nose twitched. "Um, yes, as a matter of fact."

"Wouldn't you make a beeline for a bunch of hot dogs?"

"I'd try to think it over first," fibbed the women with her lead foot perpetually on the gas pedal of life.

"Guess you're not a dog."

"How astute." She regretted the barb. "I'm sorry. I've had a very bad day so far. Let's start again. My name is Stephanie Pink."

"Rhett Hastings."

They shook hands. She'd expected his palms to be hardened and calloused, but they were remarkably smooth. Suspicious. "If you would please show me where the hot dogs are, I'll go try to find Sweetness myself. I'm sure you've got other things to do."

He shrugged. "What was that cardboard box thing all about?"

"Ms. Wharton and I have a business deal, and she just welched on it."

"Written contract? Any legal recourse?"

She started, not expecting business savvy from camper man. "No. My literary agency handled her previous book fifteen years ago, and we'd made a verbal arrangement to do the same for this one, but Sweetness took off after a squirrel just before I arrived and now the whole deal is off until I find her dog."

"That's...unusual."

"You have no idea," she said as they made their way along a gravel path. She stumbled on the uneven ground, and he offered her an elbow. She didn't want to take it, but the sooner they ended the debacle, the better. If he was a serial killer, he wasn't going to murder her within sight of a cookout. She took his arm, strong and solid, and they made their way along the path until they reached a small clearing, where a woman wearing a green apron was rolling hot dogs around on a smoking grill.

"Hello," she called out. "My, you didn't have to dress up fancy. It's just a barbecue."

Stephanie sighed. "I'm looking for a dog."

"Plenty of those around here," she said. Sliding a hot dog in a bun, she handed it to Rhett, but he waved it away.

"Dog's a runaway. Just bolted today," Rhett said. "It's..." He turned to Stephanie. "What does the dog look like anyway? I only saw a streak of white."

Stephanie shrugged. "Big and fast. I don't know much about dogs. I'm more of a goldfish person."

The hot dog lady pointed with the spatula. "Either of those fit the bill?"

Two dogs sniffed around the picnic tables, one, a slender white dog with piles of fluffy hair, and the other, a massive off-white critter with a few scattered brown patches. Fluffy dog pranced around energetically, while the other loped, stub of a tail wagging and quivering nose the size of an eight ball. Each eye was ringed by a darker patch that made him look as though he'd been decorated by a preschooler wielding a magic marker. Roaming closer to the grill, a rivulet of drool dribbled from its fleshy lips.

"Gross," Stephanie said.

"Does Sweetness have spots?" Rhett said offering the dog a pat.

"I don't know," she said helplessly. "Don't they have name tags?"

"Nope, but they have collars," the lady behind the grill said. "Mostly when we have dogs show up they belong to someone in camp, but I haven't seen these guys before."

The larger dog lifted his hind leg and let loose with a stream of pee on a nearby log. Stephanie jerked away just in time to avoid the overspray. Disgusting. "I'm sure that smaller one is Sweetness," she said. "It looks well-groomed and...respectable."

Rhett handed Stephanie a hot dog. "What gives you that impression? Is it wearing a necktie?"

She ignored the jibe. Taking the grilled hot dog, she broke it in half. "There's only one way to find out." She bent down on one knee. "Come here, Sweetness."

Instantaneously, both dogs were at her side, accepting their treats. Rhett and the hot dog lady laughed.

"Guess you'll have to take both of them," he said. He was enjoying her dilemma.

"Fine. I'll take them both and then return whichever one isn't Sweetness after I catch up to Agnes. Don't let them leave," she said, marching toward the tiny camp store. Inside, she searched the shelves in vain for any kind of pet supplies. She found nothing but one box of dog biscuits and a length of rope. The rope would do.

She plopped it down on the counter and scrabbled through the change in her pockets. Her face flushed hot, she came up with only a dollar and forty cents left over from her last airport latte. "I'm so sorry. I've lost my purse," she blurted to the teen behind the register. "Is there any way I can give you an IOU?"

The boy raised an eyebrow. "For a three-dollar package of rope?" He waved a hand. "Never mind. I'll cover it for you. Take it."

"There is no way I'm letting you pay for me."

He shrugged. "It's no problem. I'm getting nine dollars an hour."

She had sunk to the point where she was sponging off a kid earning minimum wage? "Look." She plopped down her money. "Just give me a dollar and forty cents worth of rope, okay?"

"But how will I—"

"Estimate!" she snapped.

He gave her a look indicating he'd just realized she'd escaped from a mental institution. "Oookaaaay," he said, snipping approximately four yards of rope and cutting that into two equal pieces at her direction. She slapped the money down. "Here you go. Thank you. I'm so sorry. In my real life I'm very organized and not at all the scatterbrained person I appear to be at this moment."

He stood transfixed by her stream of babble.

Slinking out the door, she handed Rhett the ropes. "Can you please tie them up?"

"Why don't you do it?"

"I'm not skilled with dogs."

"Somehow I sensed that." He bent to examine the dogs. "Well, they both have collars and no tags, so I'll slip the rope on through." He handed the ends to Stephanie, the proud owner of two canines. Two dogs, one man, and the hot dog lady all looked at her expectantly.

"Now what?" Rhett said.

"Now," came an angry voice from behind them, "you're going to give me back my dog!"

∽

Rhett swiveled to face a large bald guy with a fishing pole in one hand and a bucket in the other. A salt and pepper mustache bristled on his upper lip. Because Stephanie seemed to be immobilized, clutching the makeshift leashes and staring, Rhett decided to pinch-hit.

"Hello. I'm Rhett Hastings, and this is Stephanie Pink."

"And that's my dog," the guy said. "What are you doing with her?"

"Oh, it's a her?" Stephanie managed.

The man quirked a caterpillar eyebrow. "Yeah," he drawled out. "I raised her from a pup, so I'd like to know what you think you're doing tying her up."

"Easy, Joe," the hot dog woman said. "They thought she was a stray. They're looking for their lost dog."

He squinched up his eyes. "And you can't recognize your own animal?"

Stephanie sighed wearily. "It's a long story. I apologize. Which one is yours?"

"Cindy, come here," Joe said. The fluffy, respectable-looking dog trotted away, pulling the rope from Stephanie's hand.

Rhett caught Stephanie's look of dismay. *Goodbye, respectable. Hello, big galoot.* He tried to remember the last time he'd been so amused.

Joe untied the rope and handed it to Rhett.

"You should know your own dog," Joe said gruffly. "What breed is he anyway?" Joe gave him the once-over and Rhett, Joe, and the hot dog lady offered their opinion at exactly the same moment.

"Great Pyrenees?" said the hot dog lady.

"Sheepdog?" offered Rhett.

"Mastiff?" mused Joe.

"Who cares?" Stephanie said wearily.

Joe shot her a look.

"Uh, sorry about the mix-up, Joe," Rhett said. "Man, that's a sweet looking trout in your bucket. Must be a good twenty inches."

Joe shrugged, but Rhett could tell he was pleased. "Yeah. You should have seen the one I got yesterday. Twenty-five, easy."

"What are you using for bait?"

What followed was a ten-minute discussion about fishing, a subject Rhett had not entertained for a solid two decades, nor did he particularly care about. The small talk was a means to an end. He and Joe parted with a friendly wave. He turned to find Stephanie sitting on a stump with her elbow propped on her knee and her chin in her hand. The dog, which Rhett now realized was enormous—probably close to a hundred pounds—was giving the ground a thorough sniffing. Every once in a while he would try to lick her hand, which she snatched away out of reach. He settled for rolling on his back, steeping himself in whatever scent he'd particularly enjoyed.

Stephanie appeared lost in her thoughts, oblivious to the rip in the knee of her pants and a tear in the other, which revealed a scratch on her toned calf.

When again offered food, he declined the hot dog, but helped himself to some baked beans, enjoying the breeze that puffed along through the pines, cooling his overheated skin. He'd been in air-conditioned high-rises for so many years he'd forgotten how to be hot or cold or anything in between. Funny. The tangy beans made every taste bud in his mouth stand up and yodel. The personal chef who had cooked his meals had changed his palate the way the temperature-controlled environment had altered his body's thermostat. Canned beans? Good sense returned as he considered what artificial ingredients he might be ingesting, and he put the bowl down.

Rhett wasn't entirely sure what to do regarding the puzzling woman and her newfound dog. Uncertainty was a novel feeling also. He fetched her a hot dog.

She blinked, coming back to reality as she accepted the offering and took a hearty bite. "Thank you. I'm starving. Don't you want one?"

"I don't eat hot dogs."

"Why not?"

"They're not to my taste. Not healthy, anyway."

"My grandfather lived to be one hundred and two, and he ate a hot dog every day of his life."

"Statistical aberration. Do you want me to hold the rope while you eat?"

She handed it over. Sweetness righted himself and Rhett scratched the dog behind the ears. The animal flipped over again, offering his fuzzy stomach, his long legs bicycling through the air. Stephanie moved out of range, staring.

"Maybe that's not really Sweetness," she said. "Maybe it's just some random stray."

"He's big."

"Uh-huh."

"And he's got lots of white parts."

"I can see that."

"And he did show up here in the campground just as you were looking for a specimen matching his description."

She looked unconvinced.

"There's a letter embroidered on his collar."

"Let me guess, an *S*?"

"Hard to say. It's sort of worn away. Could be a *B* or it could be an *S*."

"Even if it is an *S*, it could stand for anything. Spot, Scruffy, Spencer."

"Spencer?"

She started. "It's a name stuck in my memory."

"A pet?"

"No, but he was a dog, for sure."

Judging by the look on her face, Spencer had done more misbehaving than chasing after squirrels. Rhett wasn't about to dig into that particular can of wigglers. "Why don't you try calling Sweetness without the hot dog incentive to see if he recognizes his name?"

"Right. That's a good idea." She put down her snack and walked a good ten feet away. The dog eyed her from his upside-down position. "Sweetness?" she called in a soft voice.

The dog rolled over, sprang to his feet, and careened over to her so fast his paws roiled up two columns of dust. She stepped back in alarm. Sweetness reared up and put his paws on her jacketed shoulders. Having finally got the well-dressed lady right where he wanted her, he began to lick her face with energetic swipes of his enormous tongue.

She made a gurgling sound, threw up her hands, squealed, and thrashed until Rhett finally grabbed the end of the rope and pulled the dog away. He couldn't help laughing.

"It's very rude to laugh, you know," Stephanie said.

Rhett mumbled an apology.

Satisfied with his performance, Sweetness meandered toward the shrubbery to pee on selected branches.

Stephanie wiped the drool off her face with the back of her hand and looked at the dog with disgust.

"Congratulations," Rhett said. "You really did find Sweetness."

Three

Rhett walked back to his trailer, Stephanie stumbling along on her impractical heels. Amusement aside, he wasn't quite sure what her plans were, but his were clear. Fix the trailer and head out as quickly as possible. The entertainment had been great, but it was over.

When they arrived at the campsite, he located a bowl from the kitchen cupboard and offered the dog some water, which he drank in messy canine fashion. He handed Stephanie a bottle. She glugged it with more enthusiasm than he would have thought.

"Where do you have to deliver the dog?" he said.

"Eagle Cliff, Washington," she rattled off.

"Where's that?"

"In Washington. The state, not the district."

"So I gathered. What part?"

"I don't know. Someplace rural."

"Is there an airport nearby?" Rhett flashed on his sweet little Cessna parked in a hangar back in the Bay Area, all sleek metal and sandalwood with leather seats. He had a sudden craving to fly her again. Blinking, he refocused. "Maybe you could fly him."

She stared at the dog, as if mentally measuring his impressive girth. "How much does it cost to fly a dog this size?"

Sweetness took that moment to gasp and hack. Ten seconds later he vomited his hot dog onto the ground.

Stephanie blanched. "Never mind. I'll pay whatever it takes to get this over with."

Rhett retrieved his laptop and used the truck bed as a table to power it on and do a quick search. "Eagle Cliff. Are you sure that's the right place?"

"Agnes Wharton corresponds only through snail mail if you can believe it, and her address is 1 Eagle Cliff Road, Eagle Cliff, Washington."

"Hmm. Well, you're not going to fly Sweetness there. It's pretty remote. No airport close by." He squinted at the aerial photograph. "Not much of anything close by, as a matter of fact.. It's just mountains. Are you sure?"

Her serrated look stopped him. She was sure. "Anyway, you're better off driving."

"I can't," she moaned.

"Why not?"

Her fingers toyed with the empty water bottle. "I sort of temporarily lost my driver's license."

"Ah."

"I wasn't driving drunk," she said with some pique.

He held up his palms. "Hey, I've got plenty of sins on my own plate."

"I just don't want you to get the wrong idea. There was no alcohol involved. I don't drink. It was more a matter of, er, rage-induced recklessness."

"Something to do with Spencer?"

"Now that you mention it, yes." She rubbed a hand across her eyes. "But I don't really want to talk about it."

He had a pile of things he didn't want to talk about either, so he focused on the details instead. How would his assistant have arranged this travel dilemma? He'd not appreciated Sonya enough, he realized, the implacable white-haired woman who always dressed to the nines and knew more about his habits than his own mother.

"Well, maybe you could get a taxi."

"To Washington?"

"It would probably require a series of taxis." He eyed Sweetness. "Large ones."

She groaned. "This is a nightmare."

"There's always a way."

Her gaze lingered longingly on his computer screen. "May I..." A hesitation. "Would you mind if I used your laptop to check my e-mail and send a message? A real quick one?"

He handed it to her. "Help yourself."

"Thank you," she said in such a heartfelt way that it warmed something inside him. He didn't want to assist this woman, or anyone else, yet he found himself doing exactly that. Odd. She logged onto her e-mail, chewing a fingernail while she perused the inbox.

"Only fifteen messages asking where I am. That's not too bad."

It did not appear she was joking.

After a minute of tapping the keys, she paused. "Does 'Encountered a slight delay, will call you as soon as matter is resolved' sound too dire?"

"Why don't you throw in there, 'Making great progress'? I mean, you did find the dog."

Nodding, she typed and sent.

The sun began to sink, bathing the clearing in long, low shadows. Stephanie swatted. "What was that? Something buzzed by my ear."

"Haven't you ever gone camping before?"

She managed to look down her nose at him, which was a feat

because she was sitting. "I...am...not..." she pronounced each sylla- ble with crystal clarity, "a...camper."

The word *camper* came out with the impact of an obscenity from those gracefully curved lips. He couldn't help laughing again. "Well, I haven't camped in a long while, so I guess I shouldn't come across as Joe Park Ranger, but those insects are mosquitoes. We're near the water, and it's dusk. There are going to be a lot of them."

She leaped up as if she were spring loaded, bringing a startled Sweetness to his feet with a croaky bark. "Mosquitoes and I do not get along. Wherever they bite me, I swell. A lot. It is not attractive."

"Well, the bats will probably be out soon. They can put away mil- lions of mosquitoes in one feeding."

She did not look frightened, just deeply weary.

"Bats. Great. Why not?" Her face went all blotchy and pinched as if she were about to cry. A crying woman? *Make a plan. Solve the problem, Rhett. It's what you're good at.* He didn't want to be any more involved with this woman and her dog drama. He breathed and contemplated how to off-load her problem, but no solution presented itself. "Love thy neighbor," he'd recently read. Sure, love them, but invite them in? Totally inconvenience yourself for some- one you'd only just met? There had to be a clause in the fine print about that.

He forced out a breath. "Listen, it's getting late and you're prob- ably tired. Why don't you stay in my trailer tonight, and you can make some calls in the morning to arrange dog transportation?" Had he really just made that offer?

Wariness overrode the threatening tears. "I appreciate that, but..."

He held up his palms. "Nothing inappropriate. I'll sleep in my truck."

Her eyes narrowed. "And wouldn't your wife or girlfriend object to having me lodge in your trailer?"

"I've got neither." He slapped at a mosquito on his hand. "At least get inside while you think about it. There's a bed made up already. I can have the water and electrical hooked up in a half hour or so, and you can have a shower too," he found himself saying, surprising himself again. When exactly had his mouth declared independence from his brain?

He saw he'd hit upon the magic word. Her eyes darted as she considered the possibility of a shower in her future. "What about Sweetness? He won't...I mean, you wouldn't want him in your trailer. He could have a disease or something."

"I'll make him up a bed in the back of my truck."

"You're very generous."

Generous? If she only knew how completely selfish he'd been with his life. How utterly and miserably he'd failed in all the things that mattered. He shrugged. "Not really."

"Opening up your trailer to a strange woman?"

He looked away. "Haven't had company in a while. I've been away." He handed her a flashlight. "Use this until I get the electrical going. I'll come show you the ropes soon as I'm done."

She opened the door to the trailer, and Sweetness bounded up the step, but Rhett grabbed his collar.

"Sorry, pal, she's not a dog person."

Sweetness gave him a brown-eyed look that hovered somewhere between indignation and disbelief.

"I know, I know. There's just no figuring out women."

∽

Stephanie looked over the giant trailer. From the outside it resembled one of those spaceships from the cheap B movies she and her brother used to watch at night after their father had gone to bed. It was white, except for the rust stains and brown striping, with a window set on either side, and two more on what appeared to be an upper level. The trailer looked as though it might collapse when she stepped on the porch, but the rustling overhead was growing louder and she suspected she'd already sustained several mosquito bites. Cautiously, she pulled open the door and climbed in.

The interior smelled old, filled with the kind of air you'd sniff in a crypt. Dim light showed wood paneling all over everything in the small living room and kitchen area. People actually lived in cramped spaces like this? For fun?

She pulled her jacket around her and discovered in the pocket the little book Mrs. Granato had given her on the bus. It fell open to one of the pages Mrs. Granato had dog-eared. With the aid of the flashlight, she read, "He will yet fill your mouth with laughing, and your lips with rejoicing." Rejoicing? She could not remember what that felt like, but it was definitely not an emotion showing up at the present moment. Something about the darkened camper, the surreal situation, and the little book in her hands unmoored her. Her real life seemed so distant, the same sensation she'd experienced when Ian died, as if someone had torn out the last chapters of her existence and substituted a completely different story line.

Nope, not gonna go there again. With a deep exhale, she reconnoitered. The inside of the trailer was clean, if slightly battered. The wee kitchen funneled through a narrow space with closets on one side and a tiny bathroom on the other. The shower was no more than a square with a plastic curtain around it and a mildewed overhead faucet. All at once, she felt every inch of her dirty, scraped skin, from the blister on the back of her heel to the twigs she was positive were caught in her hair. The itsy-bitsy shower suddenly sparkled in her mind with all the glamour of the Roman baths. A shower would go a long way toward that laughter and rejoicing, she thought, hoping Rhett could get the thing in action soon.

Near the living room was a narrow staircase that must lead to the bedrooms. It was almost dark now, so she flicked on the flashlight and picked her way up the wooden steps. At the top, sure enough, were two bedrooms. One was bare, the mattress stripped clean. Next door was another identical room filled mostly by the bed and some wooden cupboards. This one had sheets and a blanket. It must be the one in which Rhett was planning to sleep.

She sank down and slipped off her pumps. The mattress was floppy, and a bag she had not noticed before slid and bumped into her hip. As she reached to move it away, her nosy tendencies flared to life, and she played the flashlight beam inside, the light catching the shimmer of satin. She stuck her hand inside and removed the fabric, the material soft and slippery against her fingertips. A woman's nightgown.

A nightgown? But hadn't he said he had no wife or girlfriend?

Spasms of fear erupted deep in her stomach. Lonely man, making his way across country.

I've been away for a long time.

In prison?

"Steph, you're losing your mind," she said aloud. "He's just a nice guy who helped you out."

But why would a nice guy with no wife or girlfriend have recently purchased a women's nightie? *His business what he wears to bed,* she thought. She moved the bag aside, but noticed it was heavy. She peered into the bottom, and her mouth went dry.

Duct tape. Two rolls. Unopened.

I've got plenty of sins on my own plate.

She leaped from the bed, dropping the flashlight. Heart pounding, she fumbled around, snatched it up, and flew down the stairs, formulating a plan as she went. She'd sneak out while he was fiddling with the electric gizmos, and run to...where? The camp office she'd seen at the bottom of the hill. There was a pay phone there. She'd call for help.

But what about Sweetness?

She'd grab him on the way. Stephanie Pink might be running for her life, but she wasn't going to throw away her future in the process.

As she made it to the bottom step, the exterior trailer lights flicked on. Blinking to adjust to the glare, she saw Rhett making his way to the front door.

Panic surged through her. She grabbed up the nearest item to use as a weapon and crouched down.

The door latch creaked.

Her heart nearly exploded from her body.

He stepped in. "I've almost—"

It was as much as he got out before she fired the sack of flour at him.

Reflexively he caught the flour cannonball as it exploded, dousing him in white powder. Her heart sank when she realized her missile had proved ineffective. He was still standing firmly in the doorway in a cloud of white as Sweetness barreled in behind him, barking for all he was worth.

"What—" Rhett started.

She grabbed the next thing she saw, a big metal spatula.

Sweetness went crazy, spinning in circles, breaching the air like some massive, furry whale.

In seconds they were all lost in a smothering blizzard of flour.

Four

"Why..." Rhett said through lips caked with white dust. "Why did you just throw a bag of flour at me?"

She jabbed the spatula in his direction, ignoring the barking from Sweetness. "Keep back. You stay away from me."

"Or what? You'll flip me like a pancake?" This is what he got for getting involved in other people's lives. The woman was nuts. Completely loony. Love thy neighbor probably had an "except for nutcases" clause embedded in the fine print.

Her mouth tightened. "Get out of my way."

"I'm not in your way. This is my trailer, and that's my flour and my spatula."

She shook her head, waving the spatula, which sent the dog into further contortions. "You're not going to kill me, do you hear?"

With effort, he managed not to raise his volume. "You're right, I'm not. We didn't need to waste a bag of flour to come to that meeting of the minds. And would you quit waving that spatula? For some reason it's making the dog insane." He grabbed a paper bag from the counter, snapped it open, and dropped the mangled flour sack inside. "What a mess."

She edged toward the door. Flour collected in the dark strands of her hair and dusted her long lashes. "I'm going to walk out of here, and you're not going to stop me."

"Stop you? I wouldn't dream of it. As a matter of fact, let me help." He opened the door and held it ajar, letting loose a swirl of flour into the pine-scented night. "The rope's in the back of my truck. You'll want to take Sweetness with you."

Uncertainty settled around her floured face as she shuffled toward her escape, eyes still wary.

"Out of curiosity, though, why did you think I meant to kill you? Plenty of people think I'm a jerk, but no one has accused me of being a murderer before to my knowledge."

She chewed her lip, grimaced at the grit, and then wiped the back of her hand across her mouth.

"I found the nightgown." She enunciated each word with the solemnity of a judge pronouncing sentence.

He blinked. "What nightgown?"

"The one upstairs in the bag."

He didn't know whether to laugh or swear. Instead he let out a deep sigh and grabbed a paper towel to wipe his face. "That belongs to my sister, Karen."

Her eyes narrowed, black spots against the unnatural white. "Your sister?"

"Yes. I just came from my Uncle Mel's property. My sister was staying with him for a while and she left her nightgown. I'm driving this old wreck up to Oregon to meet her, so he gave it to me to return."

"And the duct tape?"

Duct tape? Suddenly it all made sense. He actually felt queasy knowing where her mind must have gone. He'd hurt women—oh, how he'd hurt Karen—but he'd never laid a finger on one. "This is a sixty-year-old trailer. Duct tape might be the only thing keeping her together."

Slowly, she put the spatula down on the kitchen counter. "Oh."

Sweetness, having suddenly lost interest in the activities of the crazy humans, leaped up on the padded rocking chair, the most comfortable piece of furniture in the whole camper, and closed his eyes, his fuzzy hind end hanging off the cushion.

Rhett pulled a broom and a dustpan from the narrow cupboard and began to corral the fine white dust into a pile.

She watched him, her hands folded behind her back. "Um, I apologize, Rhett. I misunderstood. I, uh, I read a lot of fiction."

He continued to sweep, unsure why he felt hurt. So she'd thought him a killer? So what? She didn't even know him.

He hardly knew himself. He kept his gaze down as she took the dustpan.

"Let me help."

"I don't want your help." It came out in a harder tone than he'd meant.

She folded her arms across her chest and sniffed. Tears? He wasn't sure.

"I really am sorry. I'll take Sweetness and we'll go."

"Fine." He continued to sweep. She should go. He wanted her to. Absolutely. "I hooked up the water. You might as well take a shower first, if you want. You look like Charlie Chaplin."

Without a word, she turned and padded quietly toward the tiny bathroom.

"There's a clean towel hanging on the back of the door," he called.

"Thank you," she said, her voice very small.

Methodically he swept, trying to will his thoughts into neat, sensible columns, free of the swirling clouds of regret. He heard the sound of the water gurgling to life as she turned on the shower.

Alone with only the rumbling snores of the dog for company, Rhett stopped sweeping and let the feelings barge in. Stephanie had thought he would hurt her, and now she regretted the opinion she'd formed of him. But the truth was, he had hurt the most precious woman in the world, his sister. He'd wounded her grievously. He had no right to the moral outrage he'd felt at being misunderstood. No right at all.

You ruined my life, Rhett.

I never want to see you again. I have no brother anymore.

Karen's words echoed so vividly in his memory, the tears sparking in her eyes, her face void of the love he so desperately needed. *I have no brother anymore.*

"God's given you another chance, remember?" He gripped the broom savagely when fear took hold again. "Get it right this time."

He got back to sweeping, and when the first panful was dumped into the bag, he swept again. Then he mopped the floor and wiped down all the surfaces of the kitchen with a wet rag until they sparkled. By then, his breathing was calm, his thoughts almost ordered.

"All right," he said, putting the cleaning equipment back in the closet. "Only one more thing."

Sweetness raised his head and opened one eye as if he heard the bells tolling his doom.

"Yep," Rhett said. "You need to have your paws wiped off, you big galoot, or you're going to mess up my floor again. You've already dirtied the chair."

Sweetness regarded him with suspicion.

Rhett grabbed a rag and closed in.

Sweetness attempted a leap toward the door, but Rhett held him by the collar and straddled him. Sweetness whined and wriggled, even letting loose with a heartrending howl at one point, but Rhett succeeded in lifting each paw and wiping clean the rough pads. When he finished, Sweetness squeezed underneath the kitchen table, his stubby tail toward Rhett, and licked each of his paws with sullen recrimination.

"Sorry, dog." Rhett dropped the rag into the trash bag. "You shouldn't mess with a guy who's packing a blue nightie and two rolls of duct tape."

⌇

Stephanie let the hot water wash the flour from her face and body. How could she have made such a colossal blunder? *A serial killer? Really, Steph?* But a woman's nightie. And duct tape. And his eagerness to give her a place to scream. Wouldn't most people have jumped to the same conclusion? Probably not normal people, she acknowledged, leaning her head against the tiled wall.

You spend too much time reading fiction. And not the hoity-toity variety she was supposed to either. She'd learned early on that her literary tastes were not quite highbrow enough to help her mix with the English majors on her college campus. Her fellow classmates had been horrified to discover that she enjoyed romance novels, science fiction, pirate adventures, steampunk, and the odd Western. The genre didn't so much matter to Stephanie as much as the feeling the books gave her, a feeling that there was goodness and love and justice in the world, even if it was only fictional.

Her lowbrow proclivities explained why she'd never found a group where she'd really fit in until she discovered a dozen older ladies who met at the local Book Barn once a week. The "Chain Gang" as they referred to themselves, took over two tables in the small in-store coffee shop every Thursday night and no amount of threats or pleading from the manager could dislodge them. They welcomed Stephanie and gamely attempted to teach her to knit while they talked about books—all kinds of books. It was a balm to Stephanie's lonely soul. Maybe her pedestrian tastes also explained why she and the newly published Spencer had not survived.

No, Steph. That was because he is a toad and you were blind.

She had a sudden overwhelming urge to text one of the Chain Gang members and somehow join in their conversation. It would be boisterous and unpretentious, the air rich with the smell of brewed coffee and the intoxicating scent of books. But those days were gone. She was on the cusp of something great. Her destiny, hers and Ian's.

The water ran cold. Savagely turning off the faucet, she stepped out and toweled dry. So she'd made a mistake. The important thing was in the recovery, Ian would have said. The getting up, not the falling down.

She could still make it work. Take Sweetness and find someplace else to stay the night. Call her roommate, Sass, back in New York and ask her to wire money. Surely Big Thumb had a Western Union? Get Sweetness off-loaded and take possession of Agnes Wharton's manuscript. It was a sketchy plan, but it was the best she could do. As she used the damp towel to try and brush the flour off her clothes, the streaks turned into gummy smears. With no other clothing options, she tugged on her pants and blouse.

Pulling her wet hair into a makeshift ponytail and feeling glad there was no mirror in the small space, she straightened her shoulders and walked back out into the kitchen. The smell of something delicious made her stomach rumble. Rhett stood at the stove, easing a golden pancake over with a pair of forks.

The table was set with two flowered place mats, precisely folded paper napkins, forks, a bottle of real maple syrup, and a jar of organic strawberry jam. On the floor was a bowl of untouched kibble.

She shifted, clearing her throat.

He accomplished the pancake flip. "Can't use the spatula or the dog goes crazy. I think he's got some sort of utensil fetish, but it doesn't seem to apply to forks. Sit down. Dinner's almost ready. I borrowed some kibble from a fellow camper for Sweetness, but he isn't into it."

Unused to finding herself at a loss for words, she slid onto the bench seat, jumping when Sweetness slurped his sandpaper tongue up her shin. "I...I don't expect you to feed me, especially after..."

He slid a plate in front of her with one perfectly round pancake centered in the middle, a golden bull's-eye. "I understand how you would have made that assumption. It matches the facts. I'm a stranger and I'm not a particularly warm and fuzzy one. You are dealing with some unusual circumstances. I should have realized that earlier, but the flour bomb took me by surprise."

"Thank you. You're very kind."

As he slid in across from her, the sadness on his face surprised her. "No, Stephanie, I'm not. I've been the cruelest man you'll ever meet, but I'm trying to change that."

She didn't know what to say.

"I'm hungry. Should we...say grace?" he said, uncertainty on his face. He took her hand and his fingers were warm. "Would you like to say it?"

Say grace? Momentary panic. Her boss was an atheist, her parents not on speaking terms with God, and Sass some sort of believer in the moon and stars and the rhythms of the universe. Grace? She hadn't said it since she was a young teen. He was watching her, and she felt an unbearable silence building. "Why don't you do it?"

"I don't know what to say. I googled some possibilities, but they all sound artificial."

"You...googled grace?"

He shifted. "I'm new to this stuff. I heard one that a lady said in the restaurant where I stopped yesterday."

"Why don't we say that one then?"

"Uh...well..."

"Go on." She closed her eyes.

He cleared his throat. "Thank You for the world so sweet. Thank You for the food we eat. Thank You for the birds that sing. Thank You, God, for everything."

She opened her eyes to find him looking mortified. "I know. It's a kid's grace, isn't it? I have to learn some grown-up ones."

She giggled. "That was just fine. I learned it in Sunday school, er, a while ago. I sort of gave up saying grace when my brother—" she flinched. "It's been a while." She toyed with her fork. "But you know what? After the day I've had, somehow it feels appropriate to give thanks for the food and that one rhymed, so it was nifty, I think."

He offered a hesitant smile and handed her the bottle of syrup. "Now, Stephanie Pink, eat your pancake. Then I've got a proposal for you."

Five

Rhett waited until she'd eaten her pancake, which she'd drowned in a lake of syrup. "This stuff is great," she said. "I didn't know what real maple syrup tasted like."

He ate his own pancake, with the barest smear of jam, before he cooked up a second one for each of them.

Stephanie peered under the table. "Sweetness, you are not a lap-dog." She blew out a breath. "His head is on my knee."

"I think he likes you."

"Hardly appropriate. We haven't even gone on a date yet, dog."

Sweetness relented, but he stayed alert for any signs of weakening.

Stephanie finally pushed her plate away. Rhett was amused to see that she'd managed to soak up every drop of the syrup, leaving only a sticky dribble behind on the plate.

"That was delicious," she said, folding her hands together and skewering him with a stare. "So what's the proposal?"

"Right to business?"

She nodded. "I'm on a tight schedule. We agents pay attention to proposals, at least the ones that have some earning power behind them. Let's hear it."

Eccentricities aside, this slender, dark-eyed beauty had a nose for a deal. His pulse thrummed as it always did when business transactions occurred. He lined out the main points. "I am offering to give you and Sweetness a ride to a small town in Washington, which is my destination. From there I can help you arrange a ride to Eagle Cliff." He sat back, gauging her reaction.

Her mouth rounded into an *O* of surprise. "I couldn't impose like that."

"Sure you could. I'm going that way anyway. It might take a few days, but we'll get there, I promise."

"But I'm in a hurry."

He'd expected this. "True, but you also have no money, no cell phone, and a suspended driver's license. Your options are limited."

She grimaced. "You don't need to be so brutal about it."

He shrugged. "Not brutal, just business. Wharton's novel has been in the works for fifteen years. It can wait."

Her eyes narrowed. "She could decide to go with another agent."

"Likely?"

"I would say no except that I think she somehow blames me for the loss of her dog."

"Reasonable?"

"Again, no, but she's an author."

As if that was sufficient to explain the woman's behavior. He'd not dealt with many authors in his day. He waited.

Stephanie's hair was slightly damp from the shower, curling into little puffs around her cheeks.

"So what's in it for you?" she said.

"Me?"

"Yeah. You're a savvy guy from what I can see, even if I was wrong about the killer part, so what do you get out of the deal?"

He shifted. "I'm picking up a passenger in Oregon, and it would be handy to have another person along to help."

"What kind of passenger?"

"My sister."

Her eyes opened wide. "Does she...need a helper for traveling?"

He cleared a sudden lump in his throat. "Yes. Karen had an accident. A head injury from falling off a ladder. She's been at a top-of-the-line rehab hospital in San Francisco, and then she went to stay with her friend Bethany in Oregon. I'm picking her up on the way to Washington."

"What's in Washington?"

"Karen's new home. It would have been easier to fly, but she's got a phobia. We're going to our apple farm. Used to belong to our grandfather. It needs some work, so I'm pulling this trailer up for my sister to live in until we get it habitable." It was the first time he'd said it aloud. Our apple farm. Now it was real.

She quirked an eyebrow. "This sounds like a novel."

"Truth is stranger than fiction."

"Amen to that. Is Karen single, then?"

The pain stabbed him with unexpected virulence even after all these years. "Yes," he managed. "She is."

He found that he was leaning forward, so he forced himself into a more relaxed posture. If Stephanie declined his offer, he would understand. There was undoubtedly an easier solution to her problem, one that didn't involve helping with Karen—a matter much more complicated than he could describe at present—and traveling at the snail's pace allowed by an ancient trailer.

She drummed her fingers on the table. The polish on her nails was chipped. "I'll have to insist on a couple of conditions."

He tried to hide his pleasure. "Okay. Let's hear them."

She held up a finger. "First, I'm not comfortable sharing a trailer with a strange man."

"Especially one with a stash of duct tape?"

She smiled, cheeks pink. "Yes."

"Fine. I'm happy sleeping in the truck when I need some shut-eye. Anything else?"

"Two." She ticked off a second finger. "I will keep an itemized list of all the expenses and food, and you will be paid back every red cent that you spend on me and Sweetness."

"Not necessary."

"Yes, it is. I'm not going to let anyone take care of me." There was depth in the words, echoes of disappointment and newfound determination. And toughness. He liked the toughness.

"All right."

"And I'm going to need a book soon," she added.

"What kind of book?"

"Thriller, mystery, romance—I'm not all that picky but if I don't have a book to read, I get a little edgy. It's an obsession, but harmless, I think."

"I'll see what I can find." They shook hands to seal the deal.

She yawned. "I'm really exhausted. I imagine you'll want to leave early in the morning?" Her tone was hopeful.

"We'll head to town first thing to get a part for the trailer."

"Okay. I'll be ready."

She helped him clear the table.

He picked up the bowl of batter, ready to dump the remainder, when Sweetness scrambled from under the table, skidded to a stop at the stove, and reared up on his hind legs. His big black nose quivered and a rivulet of drool escaped his mouth.

"Dogs don't eat pancakes, do they?" Stephanie said.

Rhett turned the pan on to heat up. "He likes hot dogs so I guess it's possible." When the pan sizzled, he poured in the batter and allowed it to cook before he flipped it with the forks. Sweetness hopped from paw to paw in a clumsy canine dance. When it was done to perfection and had cooled a little, Rhett put the pancake on a paper plate and placed it in front of the dog.

Sweetness devoured it in two bites.

Then he ate the paper plate.

⚬⚬

Stephanie gratefully accepted the T-shirt Rhett loaned her to use for sleeping. Armani. Another surprise. The thing would probably cost more than a hundred bucks at Saks. All of Stephanie's designer clothes were bought at thrift shops and secondhand boutiques, where she and Sass loved to scour the shelves for special finds. They still paid too much, and then it was ramen noodles and toast until the next payday rolled around.

It was pure pleasure to feel the clean, soft cotton against her skin. She folded and tucked Karen's nightgown away in a drawer, wondering about Rhett's sister—how it felt to be removed from your home, from everything familiar.

She'd felt adrift in her life too. She recalled the days and weeks after her brother died. Waking up and feeling certain, dead sure, that she would find Ian in his room with his nose in a book and a half eaten bologna sandwich on his pillow. How cruel to sneak down the moonlit hall and find he was not there, to feel again the terrible finality of it all, the excruciating stillness of his empty room. He was gone. He would never return in spite of her insistent dreams. When the ache intensified, she blinked hard and folded her hands. "God…" It was as far as she ever got in talking to Him about Ian. It seemed as though she could not get out the second word that screamed through her soul.

Why?

Those three little letters loosed the grief all over again, the pain that could not be endured. So she and God did not discuss it. They kept to silence mostly, with occasional rants from Stephanie when she felt like letting God have it. She never brought up her brother's name. Ian was the white elephant, the forbidden topic she must never bring to God because if she did, her anger might spill out like a poisonous gas.

She thought her heart was so blighted that she would never be capable of feeling any sweet emotion again. And then she'd met Spencer. She'd thought God had sent him to mend her heart. Another colossal Stephanie Pink miscalculation. She rolled over on her side and forced her thoughts to other things.

Karen and Rhett were starting up a new life on an apple farm. Who did that?

Her imagination supplied a quaint, Hallmark scene with green fields and trees laden with round, red apples. Did Rhett intend to stay and farm apples alongside his sister? Somehow, he didn't seem like the till-the-land type. Rhett Hastings. Why was the name familiar? Her fingers itched for her cell phone to do a quick Google search.

He interrupted her thoughts. "Stephanie, can you send Sweetness down?" Rhett called from the bottom of the stairs.

The dog had crept up, step-by-step, and somehow insinuated himself in a cramped corner of the tiny upstairs bedroom, watching her with his head on his paws.

"Okay, doggie. Time for you to go outside." Sweetness showed no sign of cooperating, so she took hold of his collar. As she tugged, he became a rubbery, immovable mass, legs sliding across the slippery floor. "Come on, Sweetness." She pulled with enough conviction that the dog finally acquiesced, lumbering to his feet. Excellent. Standing behind him now, she shoved his canine rump toward the narrow door. "Almost there," she grunted.

Until Sweetness made a right turn and dove under the bed.

On her knees, Stephanie swiped a hand across her forehead. "This dog has no manners," she hollered down to Rhett.

"Do you want me to come up and get him?"

Stephanie wanted nothing but to sink into that thin mattress and fall into a dreamless sleep.

"No, I guess he's okay as long as he stays under the bed. But what if he throws up again?"

"He already hacked up the paper plate when I took him for a walk. He's probably good for a few hours. See you in the morning." She heard his steps moving from the stairs toward the door. Then they stopped. "Stephanie?"

"Yes?"

A pause. Then, "Never mind." The door banged and he strode away, his footsteps loud in the still night. Crawling back to bed, she thought there had never been such a comfortable mattress, in spite of the slight dip in the middle and the curling around the edges. Her weary body melted into the musty old thing.

Only a scant twelve hours prior she'd been dressed to impress, ready to greet Agnes Wharton, to clinch the deal and hurtle back to New York before the dust settled. Now here she was, wearing a borrowed T-shirt, lying on an ancient mattress, and escorting an unruly dog back to his owner with a man she hardly knew. Should she be excited or terrified? Grateful or disgruntled?

Grateful, she decided. Her belly was full, and she was safe, at least for the moment. It was not exactly laughing and rejoicing, but surely that would come when she reached Eagle Cliff. For tonight, she'd settle for safe and fed.

She jerked as she felt hot breath against her face and a tongue swabbing her cheek. "Ewwww. Sweetness, you get back under that bed. This is purely a business relationship."

Sweetness rested his head next to hers for a moment, as if to be sure she meant what she said. He backed up and she let out a sigh. There was no way she wanted close bodily contact with this strange animal who peed on everything in sight and ate paper plates. She rolled onto her side, putting her back to him, and inhaled the musty smell of the old trailer.

Now something hard and metallic poked the back of her shoulder. She whirled around, sitting up so quickly it made her dizzy.

Sweetness shook his head in excitement, the spatula clenched between his teeth.

"How did you get hold of that?" She reached for it, but he pulled out of range.

"I'm not going to chase you for that spatula. If you want it, go ahead and have it."

She'd have to add it to the itemized list of expenses to be repaid. Once again, she settled onto the mattress, and Sweetness crept back under the bed with his prize.

Six

"Have you seen the spatula?"

Rhett was poking through a drawer when Stephanie and Sweetness arrived in the kitchen the next morning. She looked rested, clean, and determined. She still wore the black T-shirt he'd loaned her over her flour-smudged slacks. *Too severe a color for her,* he thought. Her hair gleamed like satin.

"Um, I think I'm going to have to buy you a new one. Sweetness has tucked it under the bed." She waved a paper towel, dotted with ink scrawls. "Don't worry. I itemized it on the list."

"You have a paper towel list?"

"I couldn't find anything else to write on, and besides, I once outlined an awesome business plan on a French fry bag."

"A business plan for what?"

She shrugged. "A bookstore."

"You want to open one up?"

"I did, a long time ago." She fluttered the paper towel. "Oh, I have to add a bag of flour to the list. I forgot about that." She pulled a pen from behind her ear and scrawled it down, avoiding the hole where her ballpoint had poked through.

"Never mind the spatula. I think there's a restaurant in Big Thumb. We can grab some breakfast."

"To go."

He nodded. "Sure. Ready?"

"Yes."

They drove to Big Thumb with Sweetness sitting between them. As many times as the dog tried to creep onto her lap, she fended him off with a well-placed elbow. Rhett slowed along the main drag.

"I have to go to Mercer to get the replacement tire. How about I let you off in Big Thumb to get some dog paraphernalia, lunch supplies, and maybe some clothes for yourself. We'll meet up in an hour for breakfast here at the..." He peered closer at the small stuccoed building with an old shingle roof he'd stopped in front of. "Cup of Mud. What does that mean?"

"It's diner lingo for a cup of coffee. Don't you ever eat in diners?"

"Haven't for a while. So is it a plan then?"

Her cheeks flamed, and the effect made her look like a china doll his sister used to own. Finally, he realized the reason for her embarrassment and he hastily got out his wallet. "Here. Take some cash."

"I..."

He held up his hand. "Put it on your paper towel tab."

Cheeks still flushed, she put the cash in her trouser pocket and then rested her fingers on the door handle.

Sweetness tensed, ready to bolt out the door, but Rhett held his collar. "I'll take him."

She shot him a grateful look. "You won't lose him, right?"

He made a sign. "Scouts' honor."

"That's the Vulcan greeting. Both the Boy Scouts and Girl Scouts use three fingers."

"Ah."

Her eyes narrowed. "Weren't you ever a Boy Scout?"

As if he could ever have fit into that group. "No," he said, piqued. "Were you ever a Girl Scout?"

"Practically. I was a Manhattan Maiden for three years," she said, with a shade of haughtiness. "It was a girl's group essentially the same as the Girl Scouts."

"I wouldn't have guessed it. So you earned badges and camped and did things along those lines?"

She arched an eyebrow. "It was mostly a reading club. We read a lot about camping."

He didn't laugh, a testament to years of business negotiations where a nervous twitch could cost you millions. "That reminds me," he said, tipping down the car visor. "Here."

He noticed her swallow hard as she took the ratty book.

"*From the Mixed-Up Files of Mrs. Basil E. Frankweiler,*" she read, lifting her eyes to his. "This was published in 1967. It's about a girl and her brother who run away to a New York Museum."

"I didn't actually know that. I saw a kid at the campground reading it. I paid him ten bucks for it. He figured it was a good deal because it was the second time he'd read it."

She did not seem to hear, staring at the black-and-white drawing on the cover. He wondered if he'd made some sort of blunder by offering a kid's book to a literary agent or whatever she was. He wasn't a reader himself, not by any stretch of the imagination, and if he did read something, it sure wouldn't be a work of fiction. It was hard enough working his way through the Bible.

Were there book rules? Guidelines about what books to give what people? His sister would know. Karen always had a knack for gift giving. He still had the last gift she'd ever given him almost eight years ago—a light the size of a pack of gum that turned on when you whacked it on a hard surface. Handy, helpful—a gift that lit up the room just like Karen did. Or had.

He cleared his throat. "It was a shot in the dark. I'm sure there's a bookstore in town where you can get something else. Maybe." He reached for the paperback and found it was gripped tight in her fingers.

"No," she said, tugging it away. "My brother and I loved this story. We used to pretend we were running away to the museum. We'd spend hours making our fictional packing lists." Then, more quietly, "Thank you. It was nice of you to find a book for me so quickly."

Nice of him. *I'm not nice*, he wanted to tell her. He noticed she took it with her when she got out, closing the door quickly to keep Sweetness from escaping. She did not look back as she headed to town.

Sweetness flopped down on the seat in a show of discontent. Rhett felt the uneasy tension in his gut, the restless sensation that had been there since he'd decided on a new life that would reconnect him with his sister. Fear? Anticipation? What if the whole plan turned out to be a disaster? What if she'd rekindled her hatred of him?

He allowed himself to remember the love they used to share, the "us against the world" feeling.

Until Paulo. Rhett still couldn't quite believe he had convinced himself that tearing the two apart was in Karen's best interest. He'd stupidly thought she'd come to see that someday, but of course she hadn't.

And then the accident. On the surface, the fall off the ladder was not his fault, but deep down he knew it was. If he hadn't driven Paulo away, the two would have their tiny farm somewhere, and she never would have had to climb those rickety rungs by herself. Paulo had not been there to catch her. Thank you, Rhett Hastings.

Paulo and the fall, both situations he could not undo.

But he could mitigate, and maybe in time that would be enough. *Lord God, don't let me fail her.*

Not again.

∽

Stephanie employed her savviest shopping moves and purchased most of the supplies for Sweetness from the sale items at the Pet Emporium. Leash, bag of kibble with a picture of a happy dog on the front—low-fat, because Sweetness's bulging stomach seemed to indicate he could stand to lose a few pounds—brush, water bowl, food bowl, and she was done.

With her purchases bundled under one arm, she stopped next at the tiny grocery store and did her best not to overbuy, delighted when she found they had an "essentials" aisle with everything from shampoo and conditioner to plain white underwear and neon-colored socks.

At the corner thrift shop she bought some jeans, T-shirts, sneakers that were only slightly too big, and a sun hat, along with a cheap notebook. A soft, fleecy jacket caught her eye, a garment that would never do for New York, but seemed to holler for chilly nights on the coast of California. Only ten dollars, but she didn't want to spend more of Rhett's money. The fleecy jacket would have to stay in the shop.

With receipts neatly packed in her pocket, her *Mixed-Up Files* book under her arm, and her hands filled with several bags, she emerged into the sunlit street at nearly nine thirty. Rhett had not returned, so she lugged her purchases to a stone bench near the fateful place where she had been within inches of Agnes Wharton's manuscript. Her stomach squeezed with what could have either been hunger or her building sense of urgency to get moving.

Where was Rhett? The longer the delay, the more time for Agnes to off-load her manuscript to another agent or even pitch the thing out the window, considering how high-strung the lady was.

Lured by a shady patch of green, Stephanie left her bags on the bench and strolled away from the sidewalk, surprised to find herself entering the cool grounds of a cemetery. Was this where Agnes had been visiting, just before Sweetness had taken off in pursuit of the villainous squirrel?

Stephanie didn't mind cemeteries. As a young girl she'd been superstitious, fed by classmates' stories of the mysterious and macabre. And then Ian had died, and her life had stumbled offtrack, like a thoroughbred horse snapping a leg midrace. The reality, the finality, was too much. She spent every spare moment by his grave, talking, crying, exhorting, and reading snippets of whatever paperback she happened to have her hands on, until her parents banned her from returning to the place.

It was not unhealthy, she tried to explain. She knew Ian was in heaven, and there would be no ghostly graveside communication, but in the Pink house, silent and tomblike, she could not say the things she desperately needed to unburden, to spill the grief and anger that would only drive her parents deeper into their state of trauma. In the cemetery, she had permission to be whatever she needed to be and to speak to Ian—not for his sake, but for hers.

As she walked along the patchy grass, soaking in the cool shade and the scent of eucalyptus, she perused the gravestones one by one. When she got to the impressive granite slab at the end of the row, she read the neatly inscribed stone: *Jay Peter Simmons, beloved son of M. and B. Simmons. Gone too soon.* Indeed he had been. The marker indicated he'd died at the tender age of eighteen. She started to pass by when she saw the flowers, now slipped to the side of the stone, wilted and browned. White roses.

In Agnes's car when she'd peeked in, there had been white rose petals lying on the car mat.

"She came here to put flowers on Jay Peter Simmons's grave?" Stephanie murmured. Who was Jay Peter Simmons to Agnes Wharton? she wondered. She jotted his name down in her notebook. The great memoir of Alice Wharton's life, memorialized in *Sea Comes Knocking*, had been about her consuming love for Jedd Pimm, twin souls who had carved out an impossible marriage together against all odds. Stephanie had read it cover to cover more than a dozen times, and she'd never caught the name Jay Simmons. Intriguing.

Stomach growling, she returned to the bench, gathered up her bags, and headed for the Cup of Mud. A menu was tacked to the wall outside. The special of the day was Bert's Bargain: a stack of waffles, scrambled eggs, and bacon for $3.25. Her mouth watered. "Bert, you're speaking my language." Then again, the item below was equally as enticing: Bert's Banana Pancakes with a side of hash browns.

No Rhett in sight. Where was the man? She decided to go ahead and get a table. At the very least, she could score a cup of coffee while she waited. She pushed at the door, but it didn't budge. The second time, she gave it a shoulder. No progress.

Locked? At ten o'clock? Was this some weird Big Thumb thing? In New York City ten a.m. was practically midafternoon.

Fueled by hunger, she applied even more muscle.

"It's closed up today," came a voice behind her. A skinny woman wearing baggy jeans and a T-shirt, her red hair in a tight bun, smiled at Stephanie. She hugged herself with bony arms. A pair of glasses with red frames perched on the top of her head. "I'm Evonne. My Uncle Gene owns the place. I write for the paper, but sometimes I help out slinging hash when he gives me a jingle."

"Stephanie Pink. I figured the owner's name would be Bert, what with all those Bert specials."

"Bert's gone," she said, with a sad shake of her head. "That's the problem. My uncle is in mourning."

"I'm sorry," Stephanie said.

"Yeah, me too. You from out of town?"

"New York. Just passing through, hoping to get some breakfast before we head north."

"Where to?"

"Eagle Cliff, Washington."

"Never heard of it."

"You aren't the only one."

Evonne laughed. "Well, let me ask Uncle Gene if I can cook up something for you." She disappeared through a side door. Stephanie heard a crash from inside, as if someone had upended a trash can. There was an anguished male voice and the crack of a kitchen utensil slamming onto a countertop. Uncle Gene was not in the mood to provide a meal to strangers, it seemed.

Rhett pulled up in the truck, stopping in a red zone. "Breakfast time?" he called, Sweetness peering out of the half open window. "Knock it off, dog, you're slobbering up the glass." He pulled Sweetness back down on the seat.

"The place is closed," Stephanie called back. "The owner has suffered a loss."

"That's inconvenient."

Stephanie cocked her head at him. "You're supposed to say you're sorry about the owner's situation."

Rhett seemed to jerk a little. "Oh, right. Yeah. Sorry."

She considered all the people who had said just the right thing after Ian's death. None of it had helped in the slightest except for one old lady who must have been an aunt.

You won't get over it. You'll just find a way to live around it.

Stephanie shrugged. "You're not great at the warm and fuzzy stuff, are you?"

He shifted. "Not really. Ready to go?"

Stephanie started to answer when Evonne reappeared. "Sorry, but..." She pushed the door open further to look at Rhett.

"You're parked in a red zone," she said, pointing to the curb.

"Is that a big offense in this town?"

"The sheriff lives for slapping on red zone tickets. I write the police blotter for the paper and I know of what I speak. I also did a stint as a meter maid a while back." She quirked an eyebrow. "You look familiar."

"I've got that kind of face."

Stephanie wondered why he looked uneasy.

Sweetness barked and shoved his head out the window, but Rhett pulled him back again. "I'll just get moving along out of this red zone," Rhett said.

Evonne pulled her glasses on. "Wait a minute."

"Stephanie, are you ready to go?" Rhett said.

"Sure. Thanks for checking with your uncle." Stephanie put the bags in the back and climbed in, shoving Sweetness over.

"Stay right there," Evonne said, ducking back inside.

Rhett didn't wait for Stephanie to put her seat belt on. He gunned the engine and took off.

"She asked us to wait," Stephanie said.

"You're the one on a strict timetable." He drove away fast.

"Your people skills need work," she told him, looking back.

Evonne stood on the sidewalk, her hands on her hips, staring at them.

Seven

Rhett didn't slow until they turned into the campground again. A reporter. Naturally. He was a magnet for reporters, especially now.

Stephanie kept sneaking looks at him. He parked and headed off with the tire while she volunteered to make them a late breakfast or an early lunch or whatever a person was supposed to eat at 10:57 in the morning. He wrestled with the wheel, the muscle action helping him think. He'd have to tell Stephanie eventually, and it would without doubt change her perception of him. He realized he was enjoying being plain camper Rhett Hastings, helping out a dog and a lady in need. She'd even thought he was nice—that is, until he'd been unsympathetic about Bert from the diner.

You're supposed to say you're sorry about the owner's situation.

He knew from watching other people what he was supposed to say and how he was supposed to act, but left to his own devices, he inevitably didn't. He thought of the last update he'd gleaned from his online snooping some weeks before Karen's accident six months prior. His sister had posted a picture of herself beside a little fruit stand on the edge of the field where she was a tenant farmer. He'd noted the price of the melons in the background, the ramshackle quality of the wooden stand, the faded awning. He knew she'd bought a used truck because he'd seen it parked outside her tiny rented house when he'd used Google Earth in the dark predawn hours of one particularly restless night. He'd known about the truck, and the Facebook page she'd started for her fruit stand, and the letter to the editor she'd penned about the importance of supporting local farmers, all details he didn't have the right to know. How was that possible? If he had truly understood how much Karen loved Paulo, would he have still acted the same eight years ago?

Probably, because he was a bad man. It was bad, snooping into his sister's world, and pathetic, like a dumb kid with his nose pressed against the window, staring through the fogged glass at the thing he wanted most.

Good men did not do that, keep tabs on the life of a woman who had disowned them. He wondered again why he'd been given a second chance. It wasn't out of character for God to use the wrecked. He felt a little spurt of hope. He'd noted in the Bible he'd been plowing through at snail speed that God seemed to pick all kinds of blunderers to work through. God loved bad men too, sinners one and all. That was comforting. But He worked things out in unexpected ways, and that was not.

Rhett didn't want the unexpected. He had a plan and he needed God to make it happen. God was on board for sure, or Rhett wouldn't have felt the undeniable directive to turn his life upside down. Certainly what he'd done wasn't logical or sensible, walking away from a billion-dollar empire—*his* empire, his magnum opus—but the outcome would be worth it.

It had to be. He felt again the quick, cold flush of doubt, which he screwed down along with the lug nuts. Stephanie appeared by his side, handing him a sandwich wrapped in a paper towel. Bologna and cheese on white bread.

She was wearing a pair of jeans and sneakers and a blue tank top that showed off her slender arms. Far from looking like a literary agent, she looked more like a college kid headed to the gym.

"Is this a to-go meal?" he said.

"I thought we could take it on the road since you've finished the tire."

He peered at the sandwich, feeling the spongy bread squish between his fingers. "White bread?"

"Uh-huh. Only ninety-nine cents a loaf."

There is a reason for that, he thought. He hadn't eaten white bread since he was in grade school. He considered the cheese. "Cheddar?" he asked hopefully.

"It's a genuine American processed cheese food. It's practically the same as cheddar."

"Only ninety-nine cents a pack?"

"No, a dollar and a quarter."

"Extravagant."

"Sarcasm is not attractive."

She took a bite of her own sandwich and watched him. "Before you go there, the meat is bologna, also a genuine American culinary treasure and yes, it was on sale. What's the problem?"

"I don't eat white bread and bologna."

"Why not?"

"Because it's cheap, processed food that has no quality ingredients."

She stopped chewing. "Again, this is one of those moments when you should have said something completely different."

"What should I have said?"

"Thank you for making me this sandwich, Stephanie, and for doing all that great bargain shopping. I sure am going to relish this delicious meal."

Her eyes locked on his, vibrant and glowing like pools of rich, dark honey drawn straight from his grandfather's beehives. How odd that he should remember that now, the memory of the succulent honey trickling over his senses so vividly he could almost taste it. "Thank you," he found himself saying.

She smiled. "It's a start." She held out a note. "It's from Evonne. She wants to talk to you but doesn't have your number. Someone in town told her we were staying here."

He made a show of readjusting the bread.

"Is there something you want to share besides your warped views on food?"

He pocketed the note and studied his sandwich. "What's bologna made out of anyway?"

"You'll enjoy it more if you don't know the answer."

Rhett took a bite and Stephanie did the same from her sandwich, still waiting.

The bread jammed together in a gummy ball in his mouth. Not altogether bad tasting, but not the smoked Gouda and tomato on sourdough he was used to. He took another bite and ordered his face to look happy about it.

Sweetness burst out of the camper and hopped down the steps, sniffing the air, with a massive shake of his shoulders. Stephanie gave the dog only a passing glance. "So? Who are you really, Rhett Hastings?"

"I'm a businessman. Retired."

She raised an eyebrow.

"I did well. Very well. People like to write articles about me."

She gave him the other eyebrow. "That's all you're going to say?"

He shrugged. Something about her frank stare and the gentle curve to her lips made him want to tell her the whole story, but he'd have to explain everything and he desperately did not want to fall in her estimation. That surprised him. Who was she that he should care? "At least we've cleared up that I'm not a serial killer."

"Why did you retire?"

"I've messed some things up. I'm..." He took a deep breath. Could he say it to this woman who seemed to see right past his facade? Could he actually give voice to the belief on which he was staking everything? The fantastic, unbelievable story playing out in his life? "I'm trusting God is going to help me work it all out."

There. He'd said it. Aloud. To her. He realized he was holding his breath.

"Like a storybook ending." Her eyes widened. "I used to trust Him with my storybook ending too," she said softly.

"Something changed?"

A shadow darkened her face. "There were revisions."

The silence stretched between them.

Revisions.

She blamed God for whatever had happened, he read in her eyes. In a way, he wished he could do the same, but he knew who was responsible for his revisions.

"Revisions can be brutal," he said.

"Tell me about it."

∽

In spite of her prodding, she got nothing further from Rhett, and her curiosity burned like a live wire. Ruthless businessman she could believe; wealthy, likely in light of his food snobbery, but the following-God thing? That set her back a pace. Intriguing, like Jedd Pimm from Agnes's novel. A man of many layers, and so far she'd only had the barest glimpse of the ones he kept hidden.

I've messed some things up. I'm trusting God to help me work it all out.

"Don't be surprised if He mucks up your plans, Rhett," she wanted to tell him. "God will hack your story to pieces until you can't recognize it anymore."

The temperature was climbing into the nineties by the time Rhett had unhooked various wires and coils and hitched the behemoth up to the truck. Stephanie fanned herself with a paper plate.

"It's too hot for Sweetness in the trailer," Rhett announced when he'd finished. She noticed that his sandwich was gone and Sweetness was looking particularly pleased, as he smacked his fleshy lips. Coconspirators, she decided.

"The dog is going to have to ride up front with us in the truck."

Stephanie heaved a sigh. *Whatever will get me closer to that manuscript,* she thought, cramming in next to Sweetness who didn't seem to be inclined to make himself any smaller to accommodate. "This dog is enormous," she said. "He's got to have elephant genes."

"I did some research. Brown spots aside, he looks like a Great Pyrenees to me."

"He's a great big couch potato," she said as Sweetness tried to slide his heavy wedge of a head onto her lap. When she blocked his efforts, he turned on his side, jamming his spine against her thigh and wiggling a bit, perhaps to suggest a convenient spot for scratching. She did not oblige. Rhett didn't seem to mind the fact that he had four paws pressed against his leg.

They rumbled toward the campground exit, an ominous creaking coming from the rear.

"Is it supposed to make that noise?"

Rhett looked peeved. "Yep. It's all perfectly normal."

So far precisely none of her trip had been normal. She wondered how many dozens of e-mails Mr. Klein had sent, inquiring in that polite English way that meant, "Where in tarnation are you, you ridiculous excuse for an agent?" She itched to borrow Rhett's phone again.

Gazing out the window, she noticed little puffs of dust swirling around the tires. Five miles an hour? Her ficus grew faster than that.

Hot Dog Lady tootled up on a golf cart, braking to a halt as they prepared to roll out the front drive.

"Hello, campers," she said. "Evonne just called again. She's on her way over to talk to you. She said not to leave."

Rhett waved an airy hand. "Sorry. In a real hurry. I'll try to call her later. Thanks for the hospitality."

"I'll give her your cell number—"

"No, no. Don't do that," Rhett started, but she'd already tootled off. With a loud exhale, he pressed the accelerator and they pushed on.

"Don't you want to leave your cell number for her?" Stephanie asked.

"No. We're in a hurry, remember? Agnes wants her dog and you need to get that manuscript."

Uh-huh. And what do you need? Stephanie settled into the seat, determined that she would know the truth about Rhett Hastings soon enough.

Eight

They drove steadily but slowly. Stephanie dozed, her head resting against the hot window, Sweetness snoring away beside her.

She awoke to a hard jolt, and as she opened her eyes she reacquainted her brain with the facts. She was in a pickup. Next to a large dog. Beside a mysterious man who seemed, at the moment, to be guiding the truck and attached trailer to a halt.

"Why are we stopping?" she said, rolling a kink out of her shoulder.

"Gas. This is the only fuel for another fifty miles. Better take a stretch break." She slithered from the seat, startled when Sweetness hopped down beside her. He made a move to trot off toward the shrubbery, but she quickly clipped him to a leash.

"You're not going anywhere without an escort," she said.

Rhett gamely held onto the leash while she used the facilities and trekked into the mini-mart in search of coffee for her and an overpriced bottle of water for Rhett. She figured the one with the palm trees emblazoned on the side was exotic enough for the snooty foodie, though it cost nearly a dollar more. As the clerk rang her up, she wrote down the expenditures in the notebook in which she'd already transferred her paper towel entries. He watched her closely, his head bald and speckled as an egg, his eyebrows thick across his forehead.

Her gaze drifted across the counter, landing on an old book with a rich blue cover, slightly torn. Electrified, she picked it up. "*Sea Comes Knocking*," she read. "Are you reading this?"

The clerk looked at her over the top of his reading glasses. "No. I don't read, but are you by chance Stephanie Pink?"

She gaped. "How did you know that?"

He gave her a bemused smile, revealing a chipped front tooth. "Well, if that don't beat all. She was right."

"She? Who?" Stephanie picked up the book, waving it like a banner in front of him. "Where did you get this?"

"A lady came in here yesterday. Older, long braid. Real jumpy gal, nervous, you know? She should lay off the caffeine, or whatever else she's been ingesting."

"Yes, yes. What did she say?"

"Said there might be a young woman stopping by here soon named Stephanie Pink. She said if you were to come, I'd know it because you'd say something about this book." His watery blue eyes sparkled. "All very cloak-and-dagger, isn't it? It's like a movie I saw one time."

Her senses reeled. Was Agnes playing some sort of mind game with her? "Did she say anything? Leave anything for me?"

"Yes, ma'am," he said, giving her a solemn wink. "As a matter of fact, she did."

Stephanie's nerves zinged as she put the pieces together. Agnes had rethought the ridiculous task she'd assigned Stephanie—the hunt for her missing dog and a cross-country race to the middle of nowhere in Washington. She'd reconsidered and left her manuscript for Stephanie to find. But at a gas station? With a clerk wearing a "Body by Cupcakes" T-shirt? Not really knowing for sure that

Stephanie would actually stop there and spy the book on the counter? It made no sense.

Consider the source, Agent Pink. Agnes was eccentric. Agnes would do exactly that kind of thing, sense or no sense.

"Please, can I have what she left for me?"

He rubbed a finger along his nose. "But how do I know for sure you're Stephanie Pink? Got some ID?"

She reached for the purse that wasn't there. "Um, no, I left it in Agnes's car, but I'm really Stephanie Pink, I promise. I'm her agent."

"Agent?"

"Well, her agent's assistant."

"She famous? An actress or something?"

"She's an author."

No reaction.

"She writes books."

"Yeah?" he said, disappointed, until a smile quirked his lips, the smile of a man who took his entertainment where he could get it. "You're going to have to do better than talk. Let's see some proof that you're who you say you are."

"But I am Stephanie Pink. Who else would care about this old book?"

"No idea," he shrugged. "Book collectors, maybe. Could be worth something and you're trying to steal it."

There was no sense in trying to explain that one tattered paperback edition of a title that was now in its bazillionth printing with well over two million copies sold was worth precisely nothing. How could she possibly prove who she was? "Do you have a phone? I can pull up my Facebook page and show you."

Lips crimped, he shook his head. "Left it at home today."

"A computer? An iPad?"

"Got one in the supply room, but it's against company policy to let customers use the computer."

"Then you go back there and look me up. You'll see I'm telling the truth."

He grinned. "Can't leave the shop unattended."

A reckless tide of wedding cake temper rose inside her. She was about to let loose with a tirade when the bell tinkled and Rhett stuck his head in. "What's the holdup?"

Sweetness poked his head in.

"No dogs allowed," the clerk said.

"Rhett, Agnes left something here for me. I have to prove that I'm Stephanie Pink to get it."

"Who else would you be?"

"I have no idea! It's hard enough just being Stephanie Pink."

He must have noted hysteria on the airwaves because he pulled out his phone and typed something in.

"Here," he said, handing it to her. "It's your picture on the Klein and Gregory website."

Snatching it up, she waved it triumphantly at the clerk. He shoved his glasses up higher and scrutinized the screen. "Well, it looks like you, but how do I know...?"

"It's me!" Stephanie practically shouted, slapping a hand on the counter and causing the clerk to jump. "These circumstances could not possibly happen to any other human."

The clerk looked at Rhett, who gave him a shrug.

"Well, all right. I guess it is you. You've got a sort of ferocious look about you in the picture and in real life." With a *humph*, he pulled a package from below the counter.

Her heart swelled inside until she thought it must surely crack her ribs. It was the same stained and battered box from the back of Agnes Wharton's car, the box with Stephanie Pink's future inside.

∽

Rhett took note of the clouds massing in the sky as Stephanie hurried out of the mini-mart, the box clutched to her chest. He and Sweetness fell in behind.

She'd gotten it, Wharton's story. He considered the implications. Was there no longer a need for them to travel together? Would she make other arrangements to have Sweetness delivered now that she'd gotten her prize?

He watched her tuck a strand of hair behind her ear as she carefully rested her treasure on a weathered picnic table strewn with cigarette butts, patting the box with elegant fingers. Rhett shifted to relieve an odd internal tension. Stephanie Pink had complicated his plans and annoyed him with bologna sandwiches and comments about his lack of empathy. So why was his stomach tight as she carefully untied the string, beaming like a little girl on Christmas morning?

She stopped before she pulled the string clear and shot a nervous smile at him that revealed one dimple he hadn't noticed before. He wanted to take her hand and reassure her. Sweetness sensed the excitement too, swiveling his hind end from side to side, perhaps thinking there was a game in the offing.

Her slender shoulders tensed in excitement as she opened the box, and he heard her quick intake of breath. He thought suddenly of the girl he'd dated in high school, and the ring with a tiny chip of a ruby he'd given her after he'd pawned his camera. He remembered the feeling of pride he'd felt at being able to put a smile on her face, a smile that hadn't outlasted his expulsion from high school.

"I can't be with someone like you," she'd said.

A loser like you, he'd known she'd meant.

But her rejection had been another coal on the fire of his determination to succeed. And he had. Wildly. Brilliantly. In every way that no longer seemed to matter. He forced out a breath.

Stephanie stared into the box for one more second until her body language changed, slumping, like air being let out of a balloon.

She pulled out a bottle of some viscous amber fluid, wrapped in an old bread bag.

He couldn't make any sense of it. "What is that?"

Round-eyed, she deciphered a greasy note adhered to the side. "Sweetness has a pollen allergy. When you find him, bathe him twice a week, Agnes." She blinked at Rhett. "It's doggie shampoo."

He kept his features controlled, expressionless. "Ah."

She collapsed onto the bench, and Sweetness shoved forward, tongue searching. She let him lick her hand. Not a good sign. Rhett peered into the box.

"Hey, good news. Your phone and purse are in here. Agnes must have found them in her car."

Even that news did not cheer.

He sat down next to her and, after a moment of hesitation, slung an arm around her shoulders. She melted against him in a way that made his breath hitch. "Sorry. I know you got your hopes up, though it was pretty unlikely she would have left her manuscript at a mini-mart."

She sniffed and leaned her head on his shoulder. The weight of it felt good against him. The silky strands of her hair tickled his cheek.

"That was pretty sensitive of you, up until the second part."

He smiled. "Am I becoming sensitive?"

"No danger of that yet." They stayed there for a while, sitting in the shade, enjoying quiet comfort, or so he thought until she pulled from his embrace and grabbed her cell phone and purse. "Phone's dead. Can I charge it in your truck? I can tell my boss we're half-way to Washington. That will appease him maybe." She brightened. "Yeah, a small delay only. The plan is still in place. I'm not going to let this get me down."

Stephanie Pink was back in action. Adorable, though he'd never tell her that. Rhett eyed the sky, now heavy and clouded over. "Might not get halfway today."

"Why not? It isn't even lunchtime. We can drive until dark." She socked him playfully on the shoulder. "Pedal to the metal, Road Man. We've got to get your sister, and I've got a dog to deliver."

Her resilience unfolded in wondrous fashion before his eyes. It matched his own, or nearly. "I appreciate your determination, but..."

The first drops of rain splatted down, and she looked defiantly into the sky. "Oh, do not tell me that is a storm brewing."

"Radio says it's going to be a nasty one. Good for the drought," he said, going for warmth and good cheer.

"Drought, schmout. We're on a timeline."

Chuckling, he led Sweetness back to the truck. "But I can't drive this thing in pouring rain. The tires are old and we're headed up into the mountains."

Stephanie stood, poker straight, her face blazing with determination. "It's not going to be that bad. You'll see."

A roll of thunder shook the ground.

"Noah's neighbors probably thought the same thing."

This time her sock to his shoulder was not so playful.

Nine

They drove approximately twenty miles before the rain began to hammer down in impenetrable sheets. Rhett slowed, pulling the rig into an empty parking lot attached to a broken-down warehouse. Stephanie wiped away a spot of condensation with her sleeve and peered out the side window. The corrugated roof of the structure was rusted and the windows boarded up. Broken bottles and shards of twisted metal collected the falling rain.

"This is not scenic," she said. "And I think they were lying about this drought business."

"It's another half hour to the nearest campground and I don't want to risk it."

An abandoned warehouse—the narrative opportunities were endless. It was the perfect spot for a mobster shoot-out or a smuggler to hide his stolen goods. She'd have to tell the Chain Gang about it. They'd know the titles of a dozen books that would take place in such a locale. Stephanie allowed her imagination to teeter off into that secret fantasy, her imaginary bookstore. It would definitely include a whole section on books to creep you out, complete with cushy chairs in which to read them. And snacks. Lots of 'em.

Rhett interrupted her thoughts. "We can wait it out in the trailer."

She didn't want to slog out into the deluge, but there did not seem much help for it as Sweetness was now standing on her lap, his nails pressing into her thighs, ready to exit. The truck interior was getting stuffy with the scent of warm dog. She pocketed her partially charged phone. As soon as she opened the door, rain plastered her hair against her skull and soaked her thrift store clothing.

As she struggled to exit, Sweetness yanked the leash from her hand, running in zingy circles, lapping at puddles and sprinting from scent to scent. Stephanie was coming to realize that dogs simply had no common sense. She and Rhett scurried to the trailer.

He opened the door and held it for her. After much hollering and a final piercing whistle from Rhett, Sweetness finally acquiesced to join them, immediately giving a mighty shake of his coat that sprayed them both along with everything in the vicinity.

Rhett wasted no time in pouncing on the dog and towel drying him, which sent Sweetness under the kitchen table in a pout. Rhett laid a towel on the floor of the closet and carefully hung up his jacket. He handed Stephanie a clean towel, and she dried herself off as best she could before she went upstairs to put on a dry shirt and pants. The rain thundered against the metal camper roof.

When she returned to the kitchen, she found Rhett checking the weather report on his phone.

"It's supposed to rain like this until tonight," he said. "We're going to have to stay here until it passes."

"Here? In a parking lot?"

"Here in a trailer expertly parked in a parking lot, to be precise. You've got a bed, food, and a bathroom. Not exactly roughing it."

"No electricity?"

He held up a lantern. "Battery powered, and I've got two flashlights." He handed her one.

"No hot shower?"

"This isn't the Ritz, Stephanie. If I can eat a bologna sandwich, you can skip a hot shower for one night."

She drummed her fingers on the table, considering. "But if we wait until tomorrow to push on, we'll lose practically a whole day."

He nodded. "Yeah."

"If you're afraid to drive…"

"I'm not afraid," he said, fixing her with eyes the color of faded blue jeans. "I'm being prudent. That's something that pays off down the line. Firing from the hip all the time gets you nowhere."

She glared at him. "It works for me."

"Didn't you say something about a suspended license?"

She sat back, her arms folded across her chest. "I…" Cheeks hot, she stopped. Memories of the wedding cake surfaced. It seemed like a lifetime ago that she'd actually lost control to the point of plowing into that lovely symbol of all things matrimonial. She wanted to say something to defend herself, fire off a clever retort, but her clenched throat muscles prevented it.

He looked at his feet and let out a breath. "There I go again with the insensitive thing." He grimaced, sinking down on a kitchen chair. "I'm sorry."

His face was serious, his rain-dampened hair beginning to curl in spite of his attempts to smooth it down with his palms. She noted his lush eyelashes and strong chin. "You're not used to saying 'I'm sorry,' are you?"

"No." He cleared his throat. "The Spencer thing…that must have hurt. What happened? If that isn't an insensitive thing to ask, I mean."

She shrugged. "I loved him and thought he loved me. He probably thought he did too, but actually he was using me to get his manuscript close to an agent."

"Spencer is a writer?"

She could almost smile when she thought of Spencer now, the hair that brushed the collar of his tailored shirts, the full mouth often twisted in dreamy contemplation. That was progress, that she could remember him without her blood pressure spiking into unhealthy levels. "He fancies himself a young Hemingway, a man's man. His lifelong goal was to be a master of the 'one true sentence.' When we met, he was writing for the paper and taking flying lessons when he could afford them. He tried paramedic work too, but it was too ugly for his taste. Too much vomit and blood. That kind of thing plays out much better on the page than in real life."

"Spencer sounds like quite a character."

"Oh, he is charming, and when he wanted to, he could make me feel like the only woman on the planet." She blushed at the admission. She'd read somewhere about the power of inconsistent reward in animals. It worked in people too. A crumb of devotion, a morsel of love was enough to keep her running in circles for more. Embarrassing. "He's the youngest of six children, the only boy, so all of his sisters dote on him too. 'Being a good man is a hard trade, Stephanie,' he used to say. He stole that from Hemingway, along with other things."

Rhett's expression was inscrutable, but she figured he thought she was plain nutty. She was beginning to believe he might be right. Had she really devoted her every moment to loving such a man as Spencer? It was as if she were reading a novel about someone else's life when she recalled how she'd combed the city to find the one tiny coffee shop that served Wattleseed Caffee Lattes, the Australian concoction that he'd latched on to after researching a chapter for his book.

She'd been so pathetic, pining for texts he never sent, waiting around for calls that never came. Giving away all of her heart to a man who kept his firmly to himself. How had she not seen it? How could she have been so desperate for love that she would sacrifice her self-respect? She'd craved a love like Agnes found in *Sea Comes Knocking*, a rugged man, a noble man. Instead she'd chosen a cartoon character.

Rhett still gazed at her.

She waved a hand. "Anyway, his book is one of those man against nature things about a fisherman climbing a volcano to rescue his falcon."

He arched an eyebrow. "Is it any good?"

"Apparently. He landed representation with the Jackson Agency two nights before our wedding. That's when he realized he didn't really love me all that much."

"You're better off without him."

"I know, but somehow I didn't think of that when I ran over the wedding cake and flattened a parking meter. At least it taught me not to give my heart away again, ever." It was suddenly hard to breathe. "I don't usually work things out ahead of time. I'm famous for jumping into situations without thinking. You wouldn't believe how many hobbies I've taken up and never finished." She ticked them off on her fingers. "There was metalworking, weaving, stamp collecting, and the worm thing."

"The worm thing?"

She sighed. "Trust me, you don't want to know."

He cocked his head and the watery sunlight coming through the window traced his strong profile as he studied her. "But you have this plan to be an agent. That wasn't a spur-of-the-moment thing. When did you come up with that?"

"When I was fifteen. My brother and I hatched it together. Pink and Pink Literary." The sudden pain in her heart edged into her throat, and she swallowed hard. "Anyway, except for that goal, I'm impulsive. Way too impulsive, which causes me no end of trouble."

"I think things to death, and that has gotten me in plenty of trouble too." He reached out, tentatively at first, and then he put his hand over hers, his palm warm and strong as it glided over her fingers, hovering there one moment, then two, before he pulled it away. "The book sounds ludicrous, by the way. Who would read that garbage about volcanoes and falcons?"

She laughed. "You'd be surprised."

"I wouldn't, that's for sure."

She found herself missing his touch, enjoying the rare smile that graced his full lips.

"I wouldn't either," she said.

∞

Around the dinner hour, the skies were dumping rain on and off. Rhett figured he might as well attempt to rustle up a meal to save himself from another bologna sandwich horror. Stephanie had vanished upstairs with Agnes Wharton's book and a flashlight. He did not see how someone could actually read for hours on end, especially someone as fired up with energy as Stephanie, but at least it kept her from watching the clock.

He was trying not to track the time either as he waited for a text that would cement his schedule. There was only one crucial deadline for him—a meeting at Bethany's house on Friday, pending the confirmation. It was then his plan would come to fruition, the divinely inspired plan to restore his family. A whisper of goose bumps prickled over his skin. So close, so soon.

His phone buzzed. Checking the number to make sure it was not from Evonne, he answered.

"Where are you?" Don Walker demanded.

He smiled, picturing the whip-thin Don sitting behind a massive desk that made him look even smaller than his five feet one. "Somewhere near the Oregon border. How goes it, Don?"

"You know how it goes. We're poised on the cusp of a major acquisition, and we need our CEO back."

"We've been through this. I'm not that guy anymore. You are."

"I'm not ready for this and you know it, Rhett. Fun's over. Time to get back to work."

"Don," he sighed. "I'm not coming back, so you're going to have to step up and deal with it."

"Look, I've been plenty patient about whatever this...thing is you've been wallowing around in. The 'follow God' notion was fine for a while, but now it's time to snap back to reality. Take a pill, go see someone if you have to, but I need you back here where you belong."

"I don't expect you to understand." He hardly understood himself.

"That's good because I don't. What happened to Karen shook you. I get that part, but you can't undo the damage this way."

"Yes, I can." The words blurted out. "God's giving me a chance to do that."

"Throwing away your life's work isn't going to change the past. God gave you a billion-dollar business to run. Did you ever think of that? You're going to just turn your back on that bounty? Isn't that a sin or something?"

"You'll handle the acquisition. It will work out."

"They don't have confidence in me. We need you, Rhett Hastings, master of the deal, cutthroat take-no-prisoners negotiator."

The tiniest part of him leaped up at the thought of stepping back into the boardroom, where he was indeed ruler of his domain. *That's the problem, Rhett. You're not the ruler and you never were.* He fought against the desire to line it out for Don, to tell him exactly how to handle the negotiations, the step-by-step moves that would net his company a great deal. Again the craving recurred, the desire to slide into wingtip shoes and make high-powered, adrenaline-filled corporate decisions where things were black or white. In the boardroom he was not some Spencer-like wannabe. He was a powerful man's man, and everyone who entered knew it.

But that's not what You want for me anymore, right, God? He tried to dredge up the feeling again, that unshakable certainty he'd experienced in the days following Karen's accident when he'd clearly understood her medical situation. He'd gotten down onto his knees then, praying and reading a Bible he'd borrowed from his housekeeper.

God, forgive me. What should I do? How can I help my sister?

And God gave him a plan for how to restore Karen's life. Just like that, it settled in Rhett's mind and heart with all the certainty of an ironclad contract.

He realized Don was waiting, the silence perhaps giving him the false sense that Rhett was reconsidering. "You'll be fine, Don."

"But—"

"Got to go now." He disconnected and stood in the gloomy kitchen, hands gripping the chair, breathing. *You're doing the right thing. You'll see the results soon enough.*

He wiped a bead of sweat from his temple. Sweetness clicked across the floor and stared at him.

What does a dog see? he wondered. Dogs didn't care if you were wearing wingtip shoes or flip-flops from the dollar store. They looked at you and saw the intangibles, the man inside. Rhett was not a corporate mogul to this dog. He was merely a provider of pancakes, but something in the dog's deep gaze made him think the animal could discern something more. What did Sweetness see inside of Rhett Hastings?

He crouched down.

"I've been plenty bad, Sweetness, but I'm trying to make it right now."

Sweetness stared at him a while longer, his brown eyes looking deep down, perhaps glimpsing the better man who would be visible to everyone in a matter of days.

Sweetness reached out a paw and rested it on Rhett's knee. A vote of confidence, or perhaps a request for pancakes. Rhett gave him a dog biscuit and Sweetness dropped it on the floor, licking it from end to end before he started the serious business of chewing it.

Rhett was perusing the odd assortment of foodstuffs Stephanie had acquired when he heard the sound of water dripping in a place where no water should have access. The leak turned out to be in the living room, dampening a corner of the lumpy couch. Sliding the furniture aside, he put a bucket into position to catch the drips and pulled on his jacket again. Armed with a few supplies, he readied himself to climb up on the trailer roof.

Don would laugh himself silly, Rhett thought. No, more likely he'd be calling some mental health professionals. Former CEO Rhett Hastings, the man who had built a company from nothing, corporate shark and business magnate, was ready to take on a leaky roof with duct tape and a trash bag.

"How hard could it be to fix a little leak?"

He remembered an old story about a kid sticking his finger in a hole in a dike. Had it ended well for the kid? He couldn't recall. Didn't matter.

Rhett had determination and duct tape.

What could possibly go wrong?

Ten

Stephanie lost herself again in the rapture of *Sea Comes Knocking*. Jedd Pimm and Agnes, barely out of their teens, strike off on their own, settling first in an old cabin in the Olympic Mountains. The story tugged at her heartstrings just as it had when she was a teen. For Ian, it was the rugged adventure that called to him. Somewhere between the dedication and the cliffhanger ending that left the world wondering, Ian had dreamed up the Pink and Pink Literary Agency. It was textbook Ian, a dreamer who could make everyone fall in love with his vision. He was that kind of boy, the kind who was easy in his own skin and happy with himself, the kind who could lift up others around him with the pull of his effervescence. People followed Ian like migrating birds seeking the warmth of a southern climate. He had that light of love in him that charmed the cynicism right out of others. He'd managed to convince their eighth-grade class that the best prank ever was not to fill the bathrooms with shaving cream, but instead to hire a mariachi band to follow the principal around for an entire day. People loved Ian. It was impossible not to.

We'll represent the best authors, Steph. The stories that change the world will come through our office. Can you see it?

She could not, not with the same conviction her brother did, but she saw the passion shining in his eyes, the glorious belief that together they would change the literary landscape shoulder to shoulder. Pink and Pink.

Holding the book to her nose, she inhaled the musk of old paper. The familiar page called to her, the description of the landscape lonely and forbidding, bleak as Agnes's emotions after Violet, her newborn, succumbed to an inexplicable sleep from which she had never awakened. She read the passage again where Agnes wandered the quiet cabin in the night, padding along bare floors, certain she'd heard the soft rustling of a baby, the tiny, quiet murmurs of life. How cruel imagination could be, or did those taunting echoes originate in the memory?

After Ian died, Stephanie had felt the same, awakening absolutely convinced she'd heard him in the kitchen rooting through the refrigerator for a jar of the pimento-stuffed olives he'd adored.

Why is the heart so slow to learn? Agnes wrote, as she felt the cold sheets of the empty cradle. *Jedd says I should give this question to God. I do, shouting it from the lonely, scoured mountain peak, the cold biting into me with poisonous fangs. Why? Why? Why?*

God does not reply.

He hadn't answered Stephanie either. Tears crowded her eyes and she put aside the book and got up. It was silly to be so emotional. All the talk of Spencer and the toll of the ridiculous cross-country trek were probably getting to her.

She reached for her phone, determined to send an e-mail update to Mr. Klein. Her finger hovered over her mailbox, but instead she found herself drifting to the Internet, typing Rhett Hastings's name into the search box. The sun had disappeared behind a wall of storm clouds and the bedroom was dim, so she propped the flashlight against a pillow and turned it on.

Google search.

Rhett Hastings.

Her screen filled.

Wow. Hastings, whoever he was, rated his own Wikipedia page. She skimmed the facts. Rhett was, she did the math, 32 years of age, born in Linton, California, raised by his now deceased factory-worker father, no mention of the mother. There was no mention of any marriages either, only one younger sibling, Karen. Stephanie breathed a sigh of relief. It seemed Rhett was telling the truth about his sister, owner of the blue nightgown. More proof that he was not a serial killer. Comforting. She read on, plucking bits of information like shells pulled from the sand.

Expelled from high school at age 17.

Whoa.

Bought his first movie theater at age 19.

Whoa!

Arrested for assault and lost above theater.

She sat up. Assault and a high school dropout?

Went on to purchase a chain of theaters in California and then in Texas and Utah.

She made the screen bigger when she read the next factoid. *Hastings Theaters is now ranked the largest cinema chain in the United States and Canada.*

Electrified, she hopped onto another site, a "dish the dirt" web page that might classify as more gossip than news.

Billionaire CEO Rhett Hastings, known for his ruthless practices and less than politically correct commentary, has purportedly abdicated his position as CEO. Acting CEO Don Walker refuses to comment at this time. Rumors abound that the move may hint at some internal investigation regarding Hastings's recent hostile takeover of B and G Entertainment.

There was a picture of Rhett wearing an Armani suit, eyes hidden behind sunglasses, sliding behind the wheel of a Maserati as members of the press jostled to get a quote from him. Another of him giving a thumbs-up from the pilot's seat of a small airplane.

More headlines blazed at her as she thumbed faster and faster through the search screens.

Rhett Hastings, the bad boy of the movie biz.

Hastings's take-no-prisoners attitude nets dollars and enemies.

Hastings Theaters' founder and CEO, corporate thug or tenacious tiger?

Rumors rampant about Hastings's departure.

She raced through the articles until her phone died. Her heart thumping, she sat on the bed with only the glow of the flashlight. Her pulse pounded an anxious rhythm as she tried to make sense of what she'd learned.

This man, traveling around in a busted-up camper on his way to pick up his sister, was Rhett Hastings. *The* Rhett Hastings. The Donald Trump of the cinema business.

And she'd thrown a bag of flour at him.

And accused him of being a serial killer.

With each realization her heart ebbed a little lower.

It must be a mistake. He was someone else, another Rhett Hastings, yet the rugged profile and sardonic smile sure matched the Maserati picture.

Had she really forced bologna and processed cheese on a man who could purchase her whole apartment building with the change in his pocket? There was only one way to find out.

∽

Rhett shut an annoyed Sweetness inside and lugged his supplies out the door. The rain had tapered off considerably, so he figured he might have a shot at covering the leak before it started again.

The travel trailer roof was a sloped affair, a sort of half level protruding above the lower level to accommodate the upstairs bedrooms. He had a vague memory of watching his Uncle Mel standing on a ladder trying to jimmy the levered window panels one long-ago summer, but Rhett didn't have much of an idea how to go about stopping a leak. This was the kind of thing he'd paid other people to do. And he'd probably not even bothered to give the fixers a passing glance. Arrogant. When had he forgotten his own humble roots, the days he'd spent cleaning toilets at the local theater and scraping away gum stuck on the bottom of theater seats? The days he'd cleaned up after kids who couldn't make it to the bathroom to be sick or relieve themselves?

God was teaching him a thing or two. Or three.

He had no ladder at the moment, so he found a hefty wooden crate lying on its side on the asphalt and climbed up. Though Rhett worked out diligently, he found his gym-perfected muscles were not up to the ungainly task of hauling himself onto the wet trailer roof. His father, a hard man who never encountered anything he could not repair, would have ridiculed his son for the awkward way he levered himself into position.

You take after your mother. All thumbs.

But they'd turned out to be thumbs that earned millions.

Didn't matter to Franklin Hastings, who never saw any value in the cinema. Throwing away money on daydreaming, he'd said of Rhett's favorite pastime, watching every movie he could afford to see, as many times as possible.

The cinema was a way to deliver people from their pain, their humdrum, day-to-day routines, their messed-up decisions. For a few dollars, they were transported from their own lives into someone else's. Maybe that's what appealed to Stephanie about novels. He'd have to ask.

There was something special in a darkened theater, the slow unfolding of a shared story between people who would enter and exit as strangers, but in between they would share the most intimate of bonds. The cinema let you take a journey alone and together at the same time. Why did that move him so much? Very little else on planet earth did.

Rhett made it to the roof, rain pattering lightly around him. Sliding his fingers along the slick metal, he found the bent part where the lower level met the upper one. It must be there, in that rusted wound, where the water was seeping in. Shielding the space with his body, he wiped the area dry with a towel and covered it with the plastic bag, quickly securing it with duct tape before the rain began to pound again.

Not exactly a textbook repair, but not bad for a guy who wasn't the handy type. He wiped his hands on the towel and scooted backward.

He heard the trailer door swing open.

Sweetness shot out into the night, followed by Stephanie.

"Stop right there, dog!" she yelled. True to form, the dog did not obey, plunging onward away from her.

Standing quickly to see where Sweetness had gone, he lost his footing on the slippery surface.

He toppled backward off the trailer roof. It seemed like a very long time before he crashed to a halt onto the oily asphalt. His breath was driven out of him in a brutal *whoosh*. His eyes stayed open for a moment, his vision dazzled with stars.

Stephanie's shriek echoed through the air. She clapped a hand over her mouth.

And then she sprinted away.

Eleven

R UN!

Panic flashed through Stephanie's body, fueling her sprint, her arms pumping and legs churning, as she followed the primal directive from her instincts. She'd nearly reached the warehouse when her brain chimed in.

STOP.

She didn't listen, continuing her mad dash until she careened up to the warehouse, pressing her forehead to the cold metal doors, hands splayed on the rusted walls, panting. Her muscles quivered in terror.

Go back, common sense demanded. The thought repeated itself, louder now than her stuttering breaths. *Stephanie, you've got to go back and help him.*

But what if...

Her throat dried up. Oh, could she face that "what if"?

What if the life was drained from Rhett Hastings and he was suddenly plucked away, like Ian, like Agnes's Violet? Gone without warning or preamble, without a moment to say goodbye. Then there would be the horrible quiet, the sudden ceasing of life and spirit and she could not take that. Not again.

She couldn't go back. Her fingers balled into fists now, she pressed her back harder against the metal, the tang of rust sharp in her nostrils. All her body systems felt as if they had gone offline.

Fear, terror, panic. What was the antidote? Someone had suggested deep breathing to her in the past, but this situation was way beyond that strategy. A sudden image of Mrs. Granato from the bus popped into her mind, the woman who represented spiritual common sense. Mrs. Granato would tell her to pray. That calm lady, illuminated from the inside by some light that did not shine on Stephanie, would be strong enough to pray.

Could that be the answer?

"Oh, God," she whispered, clasping her clammy palms together. It was as far as she got, but somehow, pushing the syllables past her lips brought a modicum of sense back into her twitching brain. She must not run. She must turn and face it. One deep breath. Two. A sliver of calm, just enough, and she found herself turning around.

One step, then two, then a dozen.

He lay still on the asphalt. What if he was dead? She felt the panic return.

She swallowed and grabbed hold of some wisdom from the fictional world in which she'd steeped herself. This running away business, it was not the stuff great female heroines were made of, and she happened to be the only heroine around at the present. Rhett needed help. Rhett needed her.

"God, keep my feet moving, okay?"

Forcing herself, she continued, closer and closer to the stricken form lying motionless on the ground. So still. Each stride accelerated her pulse another notch. It wasn't a great distance to have fallen...unless he'd landed on his head and broken his neck. Or ruptured his heart. Or fractured a bone which had caused internal bleeding. It was time to give up reading medical thrillers.

She found it hard to swallow as she crept forward.

She was close enough now to see that he was lying on his back. His eyes were closed. The rain had teased his hair into curls, glazing the planes of his face, strong chin, and thick eyebrows. He looked younger than his thirty-two years, like a rugged cowboy thrown from his horse, which might end his rodeo career and cause him to become a hermit until a spunky veterinary doctor taught him how to live again. She shook her head. Oy. Best to give up cowboy novels for a while too.

"Don't worry, Rhett," she said, voice shaking. "This...I'm...it's going to be okay." She moved closer, kneeling in a puddle at his side and running her trembling fingers along his face and neck. His skin was warm and satiny. Check for a pulse. That's what all the cop heroines did. And CIA agents. And reporters. It was a universally agreed-upon strategy.

Only her hands were shaking so badly, and her fingertips so cold that she couldn't feel anything anyway.

Check for breathing.

Right.

Lowering her cheek to his lips, she went still. Was that a puff of breath? Or a swirl of wind?

"Oh, for the love of tuna, it's never this hard in books," she muttered.

Call for help.

Right. Only her phone was dead. She'd have to use his. Where was it? Maybe in his jacket pocket?

She reached into his left coat pocket. Nothing.

Panic rising, she tried the other one. Victory. She started to pull it free.

"Am I being mugged?" Rhett said, his eyes opening suddenly.

Stephanie screamed. And once again her legs took her several yards at a sprint before she forced them to stop. Whirling around, she hollered.

"I thought you were dead!" she yelled, hugging herself. "It's not nice to suddenly spring back to life like that without warning me. It's creepy."

He carefully raised himself to a sitting position. "Sorry. Not dead. Stunned. Wasn't that bad a fall."

She edged closer, keeping several yards between them. "Are you hurt?"

He blinked. "I'm still taking inventory."

"I was going to call for help with your cell."

"Very practical." He shook some water from his hair. "I'm considering getting up now. Do you want to move farther away in case I really do die this time?"

Her face went hot and she realized she was standing back as if she was expecting him to detonate. She slogged forward.

"Sorry." She bit her lower lip. "I, um, didn't know that about myself."

"What?"

"That I would bolt like a startled deer during an emergency."

He smiled. "You did get some pretty good speed there."

Humiliation almost choked her. "Yeah. Well, this scene in my life book is going to need some editing."

"Or revision?"

"I'm sick of revisions."

"I understand."

"I mean, a person takes a fall and the other person runs away. That's just terrible. It wasn't because I don't care about…It's just that, I wanted to know that you were okay, but I was afraid…" She started to cry. "I was afraid you were dead."

"Like I said, it wasn't that bad of a fall. Nothing serious."

"And my brother just had a little bug. We thought it was the flu, nothing serious." She hadn't meant to blurt that out, and now that she had, she saw confusion and, even worse, sympathy playing across Rhett's face. He held out his hand.

"Come here," he said softly. She knelt beside him and slid her hands into his. He pulled her close. "You came back. That's all that matters."

Her sobs subsided into whimpers as she allowed the relief to sink in. He was okay. Rhett was okay. The rain began to fall harder as she fitted her arm under his and he got to his feet with a groan. He leaned against her for a moment, and she propped up his muscular frame as best she could.

Clumsily, they made their way inside. She led him toward the living room, headed for the sofa.

"No, I'm wet. The kitchen chair."

Though it hardly seemed the time to worry about wet cushions, she did as instructed, and deposited him in a chair, bustling about fetching things which served no purpose other than to distract her from her own ridiculous meltdown.

"Do you want me to call for an ambulance?"

He considered that, taking the towel she handed him and wiping his face dry. "I think all my limbs are still functioning. No need."

"In the books the heroine always insists that the hero go to the hospital to check for a head injury," she said firmly.

He looked at her, his head slightly cocked, moisture glimmering on his lashes, a slow, full-lipped smile breaking across his face. "Happens in the movies too, but my head is fine," he said quietly. "It's been a long time since anyone thought of me as a hero."

She couldn't hold it back. "But you're Rhett Hastings. *The* Rhett Hastings."

He sighed. "You googled me."

"Yes. You're a bazillionaire. A self-made man."

"Most of my money stayed with the company except for a trust fund I set up for Karen. I'm not a bazillionaire anymore."

"But people write books about you, and you're in the papers all the time and on Facebook memes."

"Yeah."

"That makes you something special, doesn't it? You're the man everyone is talking about."

His eyes grew sad, and for a moment she wanted to cup her hand to his cheek and wipe the raindrops away. His tone was flat and dull when he answered. "I'm a massive success. Who wouldn't want to be Rhett Hastings?"

Puzzled, Stephanie raised her eyebrows. "Aren't you proud of all you've achieved?"

"Absolutely." There was the arrogance that made his eyes sparkle and gave his words a snap. "No one else could have accomplished what I did with what I had."

"I don't doubt it. Your sister is probably over the moon about you."

He looked suddenly at the floor, arrogance giving way to sharp regret, and she understood she'd said completely the wrong thing. "I'm sorry."

He shook his head. "No need for you to be sorry. I'm the person responsible for ruining my sister's life. Good ol' bazillionaire Rhett Hastings." Such a mountain of regret, a desert full of longing in that bald statement.

She went to him then, took the towel gently from his hand, and stroked it over his hair, smoothing water from his curls and face, feeling the strong planes of his cheekbones and chin. "We all have sins, Rhett," she said quietly.

"Some are worse than others."

Stephanie wasn't sure if God ranked sins or not. Mrs. Granato would probably know. She'd heard a pastor say there was no hierarchy of wrongs. Sin was sin. It made her feel better about the wedding cake thing. No one else she knew had mowed down a perfectly lovely three-tiered cake. She wondered what the right thing to say to Rhett was. He looked so forlorn, so crushed, and it made her heart ache.

Perhaps a little joke to lighten the mood? A sage snippet from the Bible would probably work, but she didn't know any. "People make mistakes," she said, lamely. "All people."

"Mine wasn't a mistake, Stephanie." His chin went up as if he dared her to contradict him. "What I did was shrewdly calculated wickedness. I ruined the man Karen loved. Intentionally. With great satisfaction, as a matter of fact, and I convinced myself every step of the way it was the right thing to do."

"I don't believe that."

"Why don't you?" He looked at her squarely. "You googled me. You know I'm a ruthless man. You know I don't say nice things, display compassion, or care about people like I should."

"You helped me catch Sweetness, and you didn't have to do that. That's compassion."

"I was curious more than anything else. You were quite a spectacle in your business suit, thrashing through the bushes."

"It was more than curiosity. And you didn't have to give me a ride to Washington."

"I told you, I need help with Karen. It was a business deal."

Something inside her stung, yet still she felt the desire to comfort this complicated man in spite of the confusion he caused in her. "Rhett, everyone has sins whether or not they'll admit to them. Whatever you've done—"

"You can't help me feel better about what I've done." His eyes glimmered with unspoken shame. "I'm a bad man, Stephanie."

"No," she wanted to say. She moved close.

He tipped his face to her. "But God can use a bad man for good, can't He? He has plans to prosper us, all of us—saints, sinners, and everyone in between." There was an earnest entreaty in his voice that pulsed through her.

Words from so long ago, words she used to believe. Now she was no longer sure. There was no good in Ian's death, and it had created nothing in her but a black void. Year after year, she couldn't see that it had resulted in anything but naked grief and her mother's resolute rejection of God, which had slowly trickled down to her daughter. Their church attendance had always been sporadic, tapering off the busier her father's accounting job had become. Her mother had been lukewarm about the whole God thing anyway, only sending Ian and Stephanie to Sunday school when they were children. The Pinks were Christmas and Easter church attenders. Then Ian died, and her indifference turned to rage. Emotions clattered around inside Stephanie as she traced the towel along his temple. "The Bible says God has a plan for us all, I guess."

"God is going to use me to restore Karen's life, in spite of my sin," he said, clasping her wrists. The touch was electric, sending sparks up her arm and teasing her skin into prickles. He pressed a kiss into her palm that lingered there, warm and comforting, like a beam of sunshine on a cloudy day. "I'm banking my whole life on it."

She stood there, transfixed. In the pool of his irises was regret, shame, bitter sorrow, and something more. A gleam of hope and trust that did not quite obliterate the other emotions, but somehow cast a glow that overshadowed them. The situation was beyond absurd, stranger indeed than the oddest work of fiction. Could she really be in a dilapidated trailer with a corporate mogul having a conversation about God's intentions? It left her speechless.

Rhett squeezed her hand and began easing himself to his feet.

"What are you doing?" she said, trying to press him back down.

He stood anyway, close now, so close she could tilt her head up and kiss him if she wanted to.

Kiss him?

She stood stock-still while he moved his mouth closer to hers. Then he put his lips to her ear. "Thank you, Stephanie, for coming back."

He eased around her, heading for the front door.

Heart still pounding, she stared. "Rhett, where in the world are you going?"

"You and Agnes have a business deal pending." He grabbed his baseball cap. "And you've lost your Sweetness again. Don't you want to do something about that?"

Twelve

I n spite of the ache in his back and ribs, Rhett helped Stephanie search the perimeter of the warehouse, the foliage along the edge of the parking lot, and underneath every pile of debris that might possibly conceal a massive, ill-behaved dog.

There was no sign of Sweetness.

Stephanie shivered as the sun died away and a watery moon took its place. He looped an arm around her and chafed her delicate shoulders. "We'll look in the morning." He searched for something that might comfort. "I'm sure he didn't go far."

She shot him a triumphant look. "See? That comment you just made. That's compassion. You care about Sweetness, don't you?"

He lifted a shoulder. "Don't read much into it, Stephanie. It's business. I've got matters to attend to, and your boss isn't going to be put off forever."

Stephanie shook her head and snuggled against him. "You try so hard to show your bad side, Rhett, but you can't fool me."

For some reason, her comment thrilled him. She thought him a better man than he was. It made him want to be that person for her. He remembered that Karen used to think of him through a rosy lens too. The thought took the edge off his happiness. "I fool most people, Stephanie."

"I'm not most people."

Moonlight gleamed in her hair, showing the exquisite contours of her face to perfection. *That's for sure.*

"You were kind, sweet even, about me running off and leaving you lying on the ground."

He wanted to press his mouth to her cheek, to feel the silky perfection of it. Kind and sweet, so not him, unless he was with her. What power did she have over him to bring out a tender side he did not know he had? "I'm full of surprises."

"Yes, you are." Her expression was wondering, slightly puzzled.

Rhett shot a surreptitious look at the sky as he released her. The rain was still falling, and Sweetness was no doubt cold and wet. For all his bravado, he was worried about that slobbery dog. Why hadn't he returned? Had he bolted, like Stephanie, and gone too far to find his way back? He covered the unease in his gut by offering a cavalier, "The dog will be fine. No sense us catching pneumonia over him."

They slogged back to the trailer and changed into dry clothes. Rhett turned on two lanterns. In between peering out the window every few minutes, Stephanie insisted on making dinner, since the stove was powered by propane. Inwardly, he shuddered at the thought, but she managed some decent grilled cheese sandwiches. White bread moved up the culinary scale a tad when coated with butter and fried in a pan, he was surprised to note.

He checked his phone while she dished it up. A message, just one, the one he had been waiting for. His breathing shallowed out. It was from Paulo.

"I'll be there Friday at noon. Not doing this for you." A confirmation Rhett desperately needed. It was coming together. *Thank You, God.*

He released an enormous sigh, catching Stephanie's attention.

"Arranged a meeting at Bethany's place in Oregon on Friday." He braced himself and forced out the words. "Karen's former boyfriend, Paulo, is coming."

She blinked in surprise. "Oh. I didn't know he was in the picture."

"He isn't. He's been in Peru."

She stared. "So he hasn't seen her in…"

"Eight years. I…I caused him to have to leave her."

Stephanie sat across from him, and he saw the questions in her eyes. "I didn't think Paulo was good enough for my sister. They started going out when she was just eighteen."

"And you did something to break them up?"

He coughed and then continued. "I had him deported on a minor infraction. He'd gotten a job here, you see, an under-the-table-type thing, but it wasn't allowed under his tourist visa."

She thought for a moment. "I can see how that must have strained things between you and your sister."

"Severed, more than strained."

She toyed with her sandwich. "Rhett, can I ask you something that might be uncomfortable?"

He leaned back. "Fire away."

"Are you sure? It's none of my business."

"Go ahead."

"This decision to buy your sister an orchard and all that. Is it really because you're being obedient to God? Or are you trying to assuage your guilt?"

Her words stung, piercing right to the core of all his uncertainty. The sensation unsettled him and resulted in the same kind of anger that got him kicked out of high school. "This isn't about me, Stephanie. It's about Karen."

"I know you're helping her, but I'm wondering if it's mostly about you, fixing her problem to solve yours."

He gaped. "Are you saying I'm making this whole thing up in my mind? About hearing from God?"

"No. I was just wondering."

"About what?"

She shrugged. "It sounds like a business plan, all these things you've arranged. Or a plot device in my line of work. A contrived way to keep the plans moving forward." She checked the items off on her fingers. "Buy land. Arrange for Paulo's return. Settle reunited couple onto family apple orchard. And then what?"

"I haven't thought that out yet."

She cocked an eyebrow. "Really? Seems like you've got all the other details banged out."

He looked at his hands, fingers laced together.

"All I'm saying is maybe you got it wrong. If it was God prompting you—"

"It was."

"Okay, so maybe God was trying to change your life, not just Karen's."

"I think walking away from my corporation qualifies as changing my life."

"True."

Her calm perusal infuriated him. What right had this mixed-up young woman to question his motives? "And you're some kind of expert in listening to God?"

"No. He and I don't talk."

"Why not?"

"Because I don't want to hear what He has to say. I don't want Him involved in my life."

"So you're just following your own marching orders. I get it. I did that for most of my life, but I'm finally making a different choice."

She met his eyes, but her doubtful expression exasperated him. "I'm not doing all this for me." He snorted. "Actually, maybe that should be your slogan."

"What does that mean?"

"This being an agent thing. Is it what you're meant to do? Or is it a way of keeping your brother's memory alive?"

She stiffened, and he knew he'd cut her to the quick.

"Ian and I made a dream together. He's gone, but the dream doesn't have to be."

"And it doesn't have to be your life's work to preserve a plan your brother cooked up when you were teens, either. You aren't frozen there, in that time, just because he died then."

Her mouth trembled, and he thought for one terrifying moment that she might cry. "It seems sometimes like I am."

The moment stretched out, taut and tense. He should apologize. Immediately. Bringing up her dead brother just because his pride was wounded. *Apologize, you big idiot.* His pride would not allow it. Instead, he sat up straighter, staring right back at her in the way that sent his business rivals packing. "This adventure is not a business plan of mine. It's an act of obedience. God is giving me an opportunity to help my sister. It's about her, bottom line."

She arched an eyebrow. "Is it God's bottom line?"

He got up. "Thanks for the sandwich. I'm going to eat it later. You don't mind if I sleep on the sofa in the living room tonight, do you? Truck gets a little cold."

"Rhett," she stopped him with a hand on his arm. "I apologize if I offended you," she said softly. "I'm certainly not in a position to dole out advice about God's plans. It was wrong. I was curious, that's all, about your motivation." She shook her head and released him.

He immediately missed her touch. "Don't sweat it."

"I spend my time hanging out with fictional characters, and we literary types are always analyzing motivation and what causes characters to do what they do. I'm sorry. I sometimes get my fiction and reality confused."

"No offense taken."

"Are you sure? You don't look offended, but your face is blank, like you're wearing a mask or something."

He forced a smile. "I'm sure. I can handle a pointed question or two. I've been skewered with way worse. And..." An odd feeling boiled up in his gut, "and I shouldn't have brought that up about your brother."

Her mouth quirked. "Is that an apology from the ruthless Rhett Hastings?"

"Yeah. I guess so."

"Then you're supposed to say, 'I'm sorry. I'm a big, fat blubber head.'"

He laughed. He couldn't help it. "I'm sorry. That's all you'll get from me."

"It's a start, Blubber Head."

She grasped his forearm, and he covered her hand with his. In that second of contact, his ill will vanished, and he hugged her.

She forgave him. Just like that, in spite of his cruelty. He'd read all about forgiveness, and here he was, the man who professed to be following God, accepting forgiveness from a woman who only remembered Bible stories from her Sunday school class and was giving God the silent treatment. Confused, he released her and looked out the window. "I'll take a walk later to see if I can spot your runaway dog."

"Okay. I'll keep the front door propped open a little in case he comes back." She blew out a breath. "You don't think he's going to get cold out there?"

"He has a fur coat. He'll be okay until morning. Thanks for the sandwich."

She smiled. "Anytime."

He walked into the living room and eased himself down onto the couch, staring at the water-stained ceiling. Her comment still circled in his mind as he wriggled around to find a comfortable position.

Is it really because you're being obedient to God? Or are you trying to assuage your guilt?

It was both, of course. He'd felt the call of the idea taking root in the days after Karen's accident when he'd read the Bible in fits and starts during long, sleepless nights. He'd experienced the truth of it seeping into his soul like rainwater into parched ground. God meant for Rhett to start a new life for Karen, and He provided a miraculous opportunity for him to do so. The apple orchard was up for sale. Karen's injury left her desperately in need of help. Armed with those facts, Rhett built his plan with all the precision of an intricate corporate merger and every step was falling into place, which surely meant God was blessing it. Didn't it? The latest detail was Paulo, who would shortly return, one wrong righted. Another step toward the ultimate goal.

Would his guilt be eased along the way?

It would be a blessing beyond measure to have that thorn extracted from his heart. But this was for Karen and Paulo. For them, not for Rhett.

All I'm saying is maybe God was trying to change your life, not just Karen's.

Wasn't walking away from his company enough of a change? Retrofitting an orchard? He threw a hand over his eyes. Still Stephanie's question poked at him.

And then what?

After the dust settled and he'd gotten Karen and Paulo settled into their new lives, then what?

Stephanie was right. He had made a plan for that too.

"God," he prayed. "I know this is all from You. It's about Karen." He prayed about his sister and humbly asked for the strength to put the rest of his plan into action. And he offered up one more prayer, for Stephanie and the runaway Sweetness.

The minutes ticked by slowly for Stephanie. She'd elected to sit in the kitchen where she could keep a close eye on the door instead of going up to bed, but it was nearing one a.m. and Sweetness had not made his return. Eyes burning, she rubbed at them. Fifteen more minutes and she'd give up and go to bed.

What would she do if Sweetness never turned up? What if he'd found some other family to glom onto? Or been run over? Or eaten by wolves? There were probably scores of wolves on this wild coast. He was just the sort of dog who would have no idea how to defend himself. Poor Sweetness. Poor, silly dog.

And with Sweetness gone, would that be the end of Ian's dream? Their dream, she corrected.

Rhett was right in a way. She felt that her soul was tacked to that dark time when Ian died, like a butterfly affixed with a pin in some dusty, glass-enclosed specimen case. But what Rhett didn't understand was that Agnes's manuscript was the key to her freedom. She was so close to attaining the sparkling goal that she'd yearned for all those years as she hung on that pin. Literary Agent Pink would arrive, the beginning of her story and Ian's completely revised and resolved, ready to write the next chapter. Was that God's bottom line for her? She impatiently brushed the hair from her face. It didn't matter. It was her bottom line, and that was all that mattered. Rhett could follow God to the ends of the earth, but Stephanie sure wasn't going to.

Worry for the missing Sweetness made her restless, so she padded barefoot to the tiny stove. The door that separated the living room where Rhett slept and the kitchen was closed, but she tried to keep the noise down anyway as she fixed up a bowl of batter and heated up the frying pan. A pancake swimming with syrup would be just the thing to keep her awake until Sweetness returned. She breathed away a thrill of sadness as she fished out the new spatula Rhett had bought. As far as she knew, the one Sweetness had stolen was still hidden under her bed. The dog was neurotic, for sure. With an equal measure of cute mixed in.

She occupied her mind with pouring the most perfect circle of a pancake ever to hit a griddle. Ian used to make them in squares, just to be amusing, but she was not Ian. No one was.

She readied the spatula, scooping it under the pancake and flipping it. A few minutes later, she grabbed a plate and dished it up.

The door opened.

A black animal scooted through. A wolf? Something dangled from its mouth, a squashy mass it deposited directly on top of Stephanie's bare feet.

Thirteen

Rhett was upright and running for the kitchen as soon as he heard the scream. He found Stephanie backed into the corner with the new spatula clutched to her chest. A dark-colored dog, which he finally realized was a filthy Sweetness, danced before her, grabbing playfully for the spatula.

"He came back," Rhett said, master of the obvious. "He's definitely got a thing for breakfast foods."

"There," Stephanie gasped, trying to both point with the spatula and keep it away from Sweetness. "That. What is that thing?"

He caught sight of the mass on the floor in his flashlight beam and approached cautiously. At first he thought it might be a very large rat. Two little ears poked out horizontally from a bony wedge of head. The eyes, filmy with cataracts, regarded him with the barest hint of consciousness.

Rhett peered closer. "I think it's a dog. An old dog."

"An old dead dog?" Stephanie whispered. "It's awfully still."

"I'm not sure." Rhett bent toward the tiny sprawled creature.

Sweetness darted over and gave the limp mass a vigorous licking. The creature twitched.

"Nope. Not dead."

He gently pushed Sweetness away and grabbed a towel from the cupboard, easing the animal onto the cloth. He sat with the thing in his lap, examining. "It's a girl. Small and no collar. Skin and bones. Starving, it looks like."

"How awful. Sweetness must have found her in the bushes."

"Somewhere muddy for sure. We should wash her off and try to warm her. Can you heat some water?"

Stephanie stood frozen for a second longer, and then she came to life, pouring water into a pasta pot, moving the frying pan to a pad on the kitchen table, and putting the pot with water on the burner. Sweetness took this as an invitation. In a flash he was paws up on the tabletop, snatching up the pancake off the plate and ripping it into bites. He shoveled down the food with gusto.

"Sweetness!" Stephanie snapped. "You have the absolute worst manners."

Sweetness gobbled the pancake down to the last piece. Then he carried the remaining bite over to the bundle in Rhett's lap, gently plopping it onto the towel. When there was no reaction from the little dog, Sweetness poked her with his nose.

Finally, a tiny pink tongue snaked out and gave the pancake a feeble lick.

Sweetness barked and then returned to his station to scour the plate clean. He looked at Stephanie, who bit her lip.

"Oh, I'm sorry I said that about your manners, Sweetness," she whispered, "you darling thing."

Rhett felt an unexpected moisture in his own eyes.

He stared at the pitiful animal and the piece of pancake offering.

Compassion. That's what it looked like from souls with no personal agenda, nothing to gain, and only the desire to comfort. He prayed with all his might in that moment that what he was witnessing was a pale reflection of God's compassion. For the bad. For the broken. For the sinner. For Rhett. He kept his gaze riveted on the sick dog, unwilling to show his maelstrom of feelings to Stephanie.

"The water's warm," she announced quietly in a tone that made him think she'd known exactly what he was feeling. She tested it with her elbow after setting the pot down on a towel on the floor.

"One of the ladies I know in the Chain Gang does this to test the bathwater for her grandbabies. Elbows are apparently like weird thermostats or something. I think the temp's okay."

"You belong to a group called the Chain Gang?" he said, momentarily distracted from his mission.

"They're knitters who like to read. They meet in an amazing little bookstore. Long story."

He eased the dog into the water, carefully holding her face above the surface. Her stringy hair floated in ragged bunches, but she didn't move. He felt a sense of dread. Stephanie sponged away the grime. They were both surprised to discover a cream-colored dog under the mire, no bigger than one of Rhett's expensive running shoes and not nearly as heavy.

"Poor, poor baby," Stephanie crooned. "She's emaciated."

Sweetness, having finished hoovering up all the pancake crumbs, trundled over to look into the pot. The little dog struggled to lift up her head to meet the massive nose. Sweetness slurped a sandpaper tongue over her face.

Rhett lifted her out and wrapped her in a dry towel. "I think I saw a can of soup among the groceries you bought. We could try that. I don't think she could eat anything solid."

"Chicken and Stars," Stephanie said. "Nature's perfect food." She found the can and poured a tablespoon full into a bowl and added a little water. "How are we going to get her to drink it when she can't hold up her head?"

He had no idea.

"Wait a minute." She ran upstairs and returned quickly with a cotton ball from her supplies. He was not sure what mysterious functions women performed with cotton balls, but he had to admit they were useful things as Stephanie first soaked one in water and held it out to the dog. She dabbed it on the little pink tongue and the dog swallowed. Another swallow of water, and then Stephanie switched to soup. It was probably no more than a few drops before the animal put her head down and closed her eyes, exhausted.

"What are we going to do?" Stephanie said. "She looks so sick."

"I'll find a vet hospital close by, and we'll take her tomorrow." He checked his watch. "Correct that. Today, when things open up."

He caught her amused look. "It's practicality, not compassion. We don't know how to take care of a dog in this condition."

"Whatever you say," Stephanie said. "Let me hold her."

"Compassion?" he teased. "I didn't think you were a dog person."

"I'm not, but someone has to give Sweetness a bath, and that is not going to be me."

Rhett looked at Sweetness, who gave an enormous ear flap that sent speckles of grime all over the room. He sighed. "This is going to be a nightmare."

Stephanie laughed. "Character building."

He was proved right when he closeted Sweetness in the minuscule bathroom and applied the dog shampoo Agnes had left at the gas station. In a matter of ten minutes, dog and man and bathroom were soaking wet, but at least Sweetness had returned to his natural color and most of the muck was drained away.

He rubbed and buffed the dog, who whined as if he were being rolled in barbed wire, until he was mostly dry. Releasing Sweetness from the bathroom, Rhett changed again, this time opting for workout clothes. He found Stephanie sitting in the padded living room chair, cradling the dog.

"I think we should call her Pancake. Panny for short."

"Don't get attached," he said. "She's pretty ill."

"I am not getting attached. Everything should have a name, shouldn't it?"

He held out his hand for the bundle, and Stephanie gave her over. "I wrapped her in another dry towel. We're going to need a laundromat pretty soon because that was the last clean one." She stifled a yawn. "I'm going to bed. What a night. Goodnight, Rhett. Goodnight, little Panny. Come on, Sweetness."

The dog scampered up the stairs ahead of Stephanie, and then he barreled down again almost immediately with his spatula clamped between his teeth. They watched in amazement as he pranced into the living room, waiting expectantly for something.

"Bedtime. Let's go."

The dog wriggled his hind end.

"It looks like he wants to stay down here with you," Stephanie said.

Rhett gaped. "There's not enough room for two on this couch."

Sweetness gave a cheerful bark and sat.

"Well, you all have a good rest," Stephanie said as she drifted up the stairs. He suspected she was laughing.

He tossed a blanket on the floor for Sweetness before he lay down on his side on the sofa, Panny curled up next to his stomach.

"You're a lot of bother, you know," he whispered, folding the towel around her so her face was unobstructed. Her tiny button of a nose twitched.

Sweetness dragged the blanket next to the sofa, sniffed Rhett and Panny, and then flopped down, his girth knocking the sofa with a thud.

"And you're a lot of bother too," Rhett added.

Sweetness began to snore.

∽

The morning came unnoticed, and it was almost ten before Stephanie cracked an eye open due to a wave of hot breath on her face. Sweetness loomed large, tongue at the ready, but she squealed and pulled up the covers. "Go away, dog."

Surprisingly, he did.

After another short doze, she dragged herself out of bed and into the cleanest of her thrift store clothes, and then she tiptoed downstairs.

Rhett was dressed in workout pants and a sporty zip-up sweat jacket. He handed her a plate with a cheese omelet. "I'm not sure the stuff you bought is actually cheese, but it was the closest thing. There's a vet hospital about a half hour from here where we can take Panny."

She took the plate. "Where is…"

"I took Sweetness out this morning, keeping him on a leash this time. He's had his kibble."

"But where…"

He flapped his hands. "Eat. We need to get moving."

She put a bite of the omelet in her mouth. "Where is Panny?" she got out when he handed her a cup of coffee.

"She got cold."

"Uh-huh." Stephanie noticed Rhett's jacket was bulging out in the middle. "Do you have her inside your jacket?"

"Like I said, she was cold," he said breezily. "Are you going to eat your omelet or not?"

She did, watching in wonder as he cleaned and secured the trailer with Panny snuggled inside his jacket like a kangaroo baby. Wisely, she did not comment, but she did file the crazy fact away in her heart.

You're not the gruff guy you pretend to be, Rhett Hastings.

They were wheels up at ten fifteen, and Rhett made good time in getting them to the animal hospital. Sweetness took one whiff of the air as they got ready to go in and promptly turned into a mass of jelly, whining, pawing the ground, and putting on the brakes until Stephanie agreed to wait outside with him.

"Not very mature, Sweetness," she scolded. Realizing his reprieve, the dog recovered quickly and dragged Stephanie toward the nearest bush. The sky was a vibrant blue now, the storm gone and temperatures warming. She did some mental calculations. Thursday travel day, Friday in Oregon to pick up Karen, Saturday Washington, and then a stone's throw to Eagle Cliff.

She wished Agnes was a normal person with a phone. She would be relieved to know her beloved mutt was safe. And Stephanie would be thrilled to hear her say something along the lines of "Thank you, the manuscript is waiting, and oh, by the way, I'm insisting your boss put your name first on the door."

It surprised her that in the wake of Rhett's fall and their midnight dog adventure that she'd temporarily forgotten to worry about the manuscript. She remedied that by breathing deeply and dialing her cell phone.

It was almost two o'clock in New York. Her boss would be in his immaculate office, fussing over his perfectly groomed houseplants and sipping an afternoon cup of Earl Grey tea. Thursdays were dress-down day for Niles Klein, which meant he was wearing a necktie instead of a bow tie. He answered before the first ring had died away.

"Ms. Pink. How is the weather on the rugged West Coast?"

"Settled now, but it's been storming like crazy."

"I see. How fortunate. I believe there is an ongoing drought."

"That's the rumor." She tried a preemptive strike. "Mr. Klein, I will be at Agnes Wharton's house in a matter of days."

His tone was light and airy. "Color me perplexed. I understood you were to make the exchange two days ago, Ms. Pink."

"Yes, er, there was a slight problem." Not slight, she thought as she watched the dog pounce on and fail to capture an insect.

"Ah. And the problems abound here too. I have heard the Jackson Agency is putting out feelers to acquire the manuscript."

"They can't!" she blurted. "We have an agreement." If a business could be an evil nemesis, the Jackson Agency would be exactly that to Klein and Gregory, the agency that had signed her fickle fiancé. Lex Luthor to their Superman. Moriarty to their Holmes.

"My dear Ms. Pink," Klein said, every syllable serrated and clear. "We have a verbal agreement, and you know that in the publishing world that means precisely nothing."

Her heart squeezed. If the Jackson Agency got to Agnes first, would she hand over the manuscript to punish Stephanie for not returning Sweetness quickly enough? Surely not. That would be cruel even for a woman like Agnes. "I'll pick up that manuscript soon. I promise."

"Of course you will," he said. "I have faith in you, Ms. Pink, and you would not let this agency down. Goodbye." Stephanie stowed her phone, her body all over prickles. It had been a good half hour since Rhett had gone inside the animal hospital. How long could it take to examine a dog no bigger than a trade paperback?

Finally, Rhett emerged, Panny in one arm and a bag in the other. He nodded curtly to her, and they climbed back into the truck.

"What did the vet say?"

"She's old, probably around twelve or thirteen, and starved, just like we thought. He says people often abandon elderly dogs rather than pay for their care."

She shuddered. Horrible. "Did he think she can get well?"

Rhett kept his gaze out the window. "I told him I could save her."

"But what did he say, Rhett?"

"He was negative and arrogant. I didn't like him."

His tone was low and menacing. She suddenly imagined what business adversaries felt like sitting across conference tables from this man.

"Okay. Personality aside, what was his prognosis?"

"He advised me to have her destroyed."

"Oh, no!" Stephanie gasped.

"I told him I could save her, and he basically said I was wrong. Nobody tells me I can't do something."

Stephanie reeled. It was Rhett Hastings and his ego against the doctor and his? "So...what are you going to do?"

"They gave her some IV fluids, and I have some antibiotics and special food." He snapped on his seat belt. "I am going to make her well."

His expression was stony with determination. Stephanie looked at the old dog. Her stomach ached thinking about how long Panny must have lain in the bushes, unable to move, slowly starving to death. Was she in pain? Suffering? Was it cruel to try to save her life? "Are you sure, Rhett? Maybe it's kinder to follow the vet's advice."

His jaw clenched. "Sweetness brought us this animal, trusting that we'd help her, not have her destroyed. Bottom line, I can fix her. It's just a matter of patience and stubbornness, and I've got plenty of both. Now buckle up and let's get moving."

She was all on board for that idea, though she was not quite sure about Rhett's plan to save Panny. If a doctor of veterinary medicine did not think the dog was able to be saved, what chance did a corporate bigwig have? She snuck a look at his profile, strong and sure, hard lines and mouth drawn tight. Hmm. Perhaps the will to love something back to life should not be discounted. Bottom line, Rhett was turning into someone new, though he couldn't see it.

She moved Panny closer to Sweetness so the sick dog would gather some warmth from her pal. Sweetness snuffled her all over, leaving traces of drool on Panny's face, which she didn't seem to mind. It was as if he wished to sponge away all the remnants of Panny's visit to the doctor who had no hope for her. *You go, Sweetness.*

Stephanie checked her watch. Eleven thirty. She mentally recalculated her priority list.

Save Panny's life.
Meet Karen.
Stop at the apple orchard.
Return Sweetness.
Get the manuscript.
It seemed the plot line had been revised. Again.

Though the panicked need to get to Washington still bubbled inside her, Stephanie tipped her head to the sunshine and felt the warmth deep inside. The dogs seemed to feel it too, stretching to catch the rays beaming through the windshield. There was no worry about tomorrow in these two. For now they were together, comfortable and warm, and that was enough. She tucked the blanket around Panny and gave Sweetness a scratch on his well-padded side. His lips curled into what looked very much like a doggie smile.

We'll have you home soon, Sweetness. And what a story we'll have to tell Agnes.

Fourteen

They passed into Oregon at sundown. Stephanie crawled out of the truck and stretched while Rhett hooked up the trailer—at a campground this time. He said it was so Stephanie could have a hot shower, but secretly he craved one too. His back was still aching after the tumble off the roof, and he didn't want Panny to spend the night in a cold room. It felt luxurious to be able to flip on the lights and set the heater on low to combat the evening coastal chill. Stephanie scurried off to run some laundry through coin-operated machinery.

That gave Rhett some alone time with his thoughts. He still wasn't completely sure why he'd marched out of that vet's office, blowing off the advice of a trained professional. Partly it was the stubborn streak in him that activated whenever someone challenged him, but it was something more than that. He didn't want to think it out, to dismantle and examine his own motivation. Stephanie probably already knew why he'd acted the way he did, with all her talk about what drives characters and such drivel. She wanted

to see the heroic side of Rhett Hastings, but it was probably simple stubbornness more than anything else.

What Stephanie thought of him mattered, but his need to rescue Panny had nothing to do with that. The bare bones of it was that he wanted to save the dog since the moment he'd witnessed the tender offer of a bite of pancake, the pure compassion of one living thing toward another. He'd never seen anything like it except in movies and, though he'd never admit it, those sappy cinematic moments always made him tear up. He really was turning into a blubber head.

"Just don't let it take you away from your plan. God's plan," he muttered to himself. He got Panny settled on a corner of the couch, Sweetness keeping a watchful eye on her.

When he had showered and shaved, he went to the kitchen to offer Panny a mouthful of the special food the doctor had provided. It was soft and smelled like a cross between beef stew and cardboard. He gave her a pep talk, which she listened to with filmy eyes fixed in the direction of his voice. She managed only a bite, but in his mind it was a good, hefty one. He took her outside and held her up to see if she needed to go. She tinkled a little, and he felt like doing a fist pump. Instead, he said quietly, "That's a girl, Panny. We'll show 'em." He was celebrating over a squirt of pee now?

Sweetness happily took care of his business, and Rhett was careful to be sure the wily dog did not stray.

Stephanie returned. "Our clothes are in the dryer. There were two guys in the laundry room watching a fishing show on this incredibly old black-and-white TV, and they promised me that no one will steal our things. Should I believe them?"

"Guys who watch fishing shows are trustworthy."

"That's what I thought too." She handed him his phone. "It was in your pants pocket. It's been buzzing on and off for a while. I think it's Evonne."

"Evonne who?"

"The reporter from Big Thumb."

He deleted the messages without reading them. "She's persistent. I'll give her that."

Stephanie rolled her eyes. "No wonder the press doesn't like you."

"I don't like them either."

"It wouldn't hurt to call her."

"I'm busy. I have to be at Bethany's tomorrow."

"For the big reunion?"

"You make it sound like a novel. I visited Karen when I could during her hospital stay and her stint in rehab."

"I meant with Paulo."

"Oh. Yes."

"They've been separated a long while."

"Not so long. Only eight years. He hasn't remarried. Doesn't even have a steady job. He'll be happy to see her."

Stephanie scratched Sweetness behind his ears. Her silence was telling.

"He will be glad," Rhett repeated firmly. "He's back in the U.S. on a work visa and starting the process of becoming a citizen. He's going to put down roots here."

"And Karen?"

"She's never stopped loving him."

"Why do I feel like you want to add 'even though he doesn't deserve it'?"

"He doesn't," Rhett growled, wishing immediately that he hadn't.

"But she loves him anyway." Stephanie sighed. "Such is the stuff great novels are made of. You should read Agnes Wharton's book. There is one part where Jedd has been off on a drinking binge and he gets robbed, losing all the money he'd earned for the month. She forgives him because she knows he's grieving for their baby."

"Did it ever occur to you that you are too much in love with books?"

"I didn't think that was possible."

There was such an earnest look on her face that he had to laugh. "You should open a bookstore."

"That's what I'm going to do after I retire from the literary agency."

"Long time to wait."

"I'm a pro at holding on to dreams for an eternity, remember?"

What a waste that is, he thought. This vibrant, intelligent woman couldn't see that she was not living her life but someone else's. He would make a note on his cell phone to remind himself to pray for her, though he didn't think he'd need it. He still hadn't gotten into the habit of thinking regularly about others, but Stephanie cropped up in his mind almost constantly.

She held up a bag. "The camp store was still open. I bought dinner. My treat."

He did not hide a look of dread.

"Oh, don't be such a food snob. You'll like it. I promise." She sucked in a deep breath. "I can almost smell the ocean from here. Do you want to have dinner outside?"

"No," he said before thinking. "I don't want Panny to get cold, and she's too fragile to leave alone."

"All right," she said, sweeping past him. He was relieved that she didn't make a crack about his attachment to the old dog until she said, "Marshmallow," as she passed him.

He'd been called a lot of names in his day, but Marshmallow was a first. Somehow, it did not seem to bother him as much as it would have before the crazy adventure started. She'd been able to see more of him than anyone else had, right down to the real, unvarnished parts.

Tucking Panny under his arm, he followed her inside to discover what culinary disaster she had in mind. Oddly, that thought did not seem to bother him much either.

∞

Stephanie slept fitfully, in spite of her satisfying dinner of raviolis from the can, which, she pointed out to Rhett, was prepared by a real live chef, as proved by the picture on the label. Rhett had eaten enough to be polite and supplemented his dinner with several slices of the fresh baked bread she'd been thrilled to purchase. Marge, the camp store manager, was quite the baker.

At sunrise it was a quick breakfast of toast for both of them, kibble for Sweetness, and two tiny mouthfuls of food for Panny.

"Two bites!" Rhett boomed as if he was extolling the launch of an IPO. "Two."

She laughed. The lightness inside belied her circumstances. "Way to go, Panny and Dr. Rhett," she said, as they packed up the trailer. "You have skills outside the boardroom too."

"Don't I know it." He opened the truck door for her and the dogs. "Ready to go meet my sister?"

"Absolutely."

∽

Rhett guided the truck along Interstate 5. Stephanie occupied herself by making notes in her journal about the wacky adventure to share with the Chain Gang back home.

A thought struck her and she jotted it down.

"Inspiration?" Rhett said.

"I was thinking of suggesting to the guy who runs the bookstore back in New York that he should put up some maps in the travel section where customers could mark where they'd been and post some quick thoughts about their trip."

"Is Bookstore Owner likely to listen to you?"

"No," she said with a sigh. "But a girl can dream."

She watched with interest as he left the interstate and took a different route, which led them along the Oregon coast. The rugged black cliffs and water bluer than she could have imagined took her breath away, a scenic postcard unrolling before her eyes.

Sweetness pushed his big head out the window and snuffled up some sea air.

"It's gorgeous," she breathed.

"Yeah," he said, somewhat distractedly. She looked closer. He was absently stroking Panny with one hand, his brow furrowed into deep lines. He was, in a word, worried.

For all his bold talk, he wasn't sure how the meeting would go between Paulo and Karen, she intuited. She didn't blame him. Love was a hard animal to understand. Like Sweetness, it was unpredictable, nonsensical, and never completely well behaved, and Rhett was deluded to think he could manage it like a business deal. How could such a brilliant man be so ignorant?

The closer they got to their destination, the quieter he became. As the hours passed, his tension began to mingle with hers as the task before her pressed in. The Jackson Agency was sniffing around Stephanie's manuscript. What if they'd gotten to Agnes already? What if this stop to pick up Karen would be the difference between success and failure?

She thought about other options. She could try to find another ride, a taxi, a plane, or even hitchhike. But there was something bordering on fear in the pinched lines around Rhett's mouth that made her feel as though he needed her. She shifted. Crazy thought. What difference could she possibly make in the situation? A stranger in the middle of Rhett's odd family scenario.

He looked at her then, took her hand, and squeezed. "I, uh, I appreciate you making this stop with me."

She squeezed back, surprised. "Our business deal."

"Yeah," he said with a shrug. "Anyway, I just wanted to say that."

She tugged playfully on his arm. "I hope your sister likes dogs."

He smiled. "My sister likes anything that breathes, the sicker and lamer the better."

"Then she's going to love Panny."

The old dog took that moment to yawn. The movement caught the attention of Sweetness, who administered a thorough examination. Stephanie shook her head. "It's like he's the big brother or something. Sooner or later she's going to get tired of it, and he'll have to stop."

Rhett looked at Sweetness, a tender smile on his lips. "Oh, I don't think he'll ever stop trying to be her big brother."

Was that what Rhett saw in Panny and Sweetness? Siblings trying to protect each other?

Sorrow rose up inside her. How she wished she had been able to protect her brother from the meningitis that had ended his life, a ridiculous invisible bacteria, tiny as a pinhead, powerful as a loaded gun. She wondered suddenly how Sweetness would feel if Panny didn't make it. And what about their inevitable separation when Agnes took possession of her dog once again? Would Sweetness pine for Panny? Grieve her loss?

Sweetness settled down again, side by side with his newfound sister.

In that moment, she felt a firm desire take root. Panny would live. She and Rhett would see to it together, and Agnes Wharton was going to ensure that the dogs remained together for the rest of their lives. The fairy-tale ending was just as improbable as Rhett's forced reunion of Paulo and Karen. Still, she'd always loved a good fairy tale.

Agnes might be addled and strong willed, but she was no match for the determination that swept through Stephanie Pink. Manuscript and dogs would be changing hands in a matter of days without interference from the Jackson Agency or anyone else. So sayeth Stephanie Pink, soon to be Agent Pink, slayer of wedding cakes.

Agnes Wharton, you've met your match.

∽

They arrived at an older, ranch-style home in a quiet suburban neighborhood. It wasn't far from the beach, and the scent of the sea hung in the air. Rhett's pulse pounded as he parked the truck and trailer on the street. Wrapping Panny in a towel, he handed her to Stephanie and clipped Sweetness to the leash. He checked his watch. "We have an hour before Paulo arrives."

He marched toward the door, and they were let into the house by a redheaded lady wearing jeans and a denim shirt who greeted Rhett with a hug and pumped Stephanie's hand. "Come on out back," she said. "Karen's parked in her favorite spot." They were nearly to the sliding door when Bethany pulled Rhett aside.

"Is Paulo still coming?"

"Yes."

"It's a mistake, Rhett."

He patted her hand on his arm and tried to keep the irritation from his voice. "It's going to be okay." Without giving her a chance to disagree, he made his way to a neat patio complete with cushioned chairs and a burbling fountain.

Karen sat in a patch of sunlight, framed by a leggy flowering shrub. He was pleased to see that her cheeks were a bit fuller, and she looked more rested than the last time he'd visited. Her long blond hair was pulled back in a ponytail.

He went to greet her. "Hey, sis."

Her smile lit up her face in a way that made his heart both grieve and rejoice. "Hiya, big brother."

He swallowed hard as she kissed him on both cheeks. "This is my friend Stephanie."

"Hi, Stephanie. I hope Rhett has been treating you well. He can be grouchy, but he's a teddy bear deep down."

Karen's friendly manner with her estranged brother no doubt confused Stephanie. She smiled and shot a look at him. He should have told her the complete truth earlier. Why hadn't he been man enough?

Stephanie introduced Panny, and Karen demanded to see her, taking the little creature on her lap. She began to coo softly to the dog.

Rhett stepped closer to Stephanie and drew her away a step. "Karen lost some of her memory in the accident."

Stephanie's eyes rounded. "She doesn't remember your... disagreement?"

He held her eyes, tried to read the emotion shimmering there. "No."

"Your sister doesn't remember what you did?"

He couldn't look away, though he wanted to. "I wanted to tell her, so many times, but..."

"But you didn't." The truth sounded hard and ugly.

"No." He swallowed hard. "I didn't. Not yet. I tried, but I just couldn't get the words out."

"Does she remember Paulo?" Stephanie whispered, while Sweetness butted Karen's hand, trying to get her attention.

"Yes," he hastened to say. "I mean, she didn't at first, but I've shown her pictures and told her about him. She remembers now." *Some of it,* his conscience added.

Stephanie's eyes were filled with profound disappointment.

"It's going to be okay," he said. "Paulo will tell her, and it will be brutally honest coming from him."

Stephanie closed her eyes for a moment as if she felt a pain deep down.

"Are you Rhett's wife?" Karen called.

Stephanie blushed a rosy red. "Uh, no."

"I told you she is my friend," Rhett put in.

Karen sighed. "That's right, you did. My head feels like it's filled with wet cotton sometimes." She stroked the dog in her lap.

"You're doing well, Karen. The doctors are pleased. How's the strength in your legs?"

"Good. Bethany takes great care of me and reminds me to use the cane. It's a big improvement from the walker. All this coastal air has fixed me right up. I'm ready to go to the orchard and get working."

His heart leaped. She remembered the plan he'd gone over with her so many times during his visits. "We can leave tomorrow morning. We'll be there by sundown if we push it."

"Finally." Karen stroked Panny and patted Sweetness simultaneously. "I can picture it so clearly. And the smell. Remember the scent of the apple blossoms, Rhett? It was like God perfumed the air."

He nodded. "I remember."

"And the little house where we slept on the floor." She looked at Stephanie. "We slept on foam mats, but I never remember being uncomfortable at all. Gran and Gramps would wake us up every morning with eggs and bacon and buttered grits."

"The days before cholesterol," Rhett said.

She laughed. "We had fun there. Mom and Dad used to send us to the orchard in the summertime until Mom left." Her face clouded. "They divorced, and we didn't go for a while because Dad needed us at home. And then the orchard was sold." She sighed. "Just like that. Everything changed. I've sure missed that old house."

"Remember, I told you the house is in disrepair. The Realtor told me the roof needs work and some of the flooring has to be replaced. I brought the trailer so you can live in it while I have the repairs done."

She nodded. "I don't care if I'm living in a tent. I can't wait to be back there."

"Who's ready for dinner?" Bethany called.

Karen leaned in. "We'd better go. She's a stickler for prompt dining."

Stephanie took the dogs, and Rhett handed Karen her cane and offered his arm. They walked back into the house. Rhett avoided looking at Stephanie. He knew exactly what she was thinking.

Karen doesn't remember what you did, Rhett. How could you let your sister believe a lie?

Fifteen

Stephanie could hardly taste the chicken piccata, though she was sure it must be good. It was as if she were sitting through some odd scene in a movie or book, Karen prattling on in adoration of her brother, who she did not remember separating her from the man she loved. At any moment Paulo would walk through the door and drop the truth of her brother's betrayal like a bomb. In a sappy romance novel, they would rekindle their love at first glance. In a literary novel, it would turn to disaster.

Rhett, she understood now, was hoping for that happy-ever-after, romance-novel ending for his sister and Paulo. Karen might hate Rhett all over again when she remembered his betrayal, but Rhett was willing to risk it. Rhett thought God was helping him orchestrate a reunion that would mend the broken pieces together, to heal her life and rectify his own sin. Could it be that simple? Could Rhett simply revise the story through careful planning and meticulously drawn strategy? Stephanie's stomach was knotted, and she could tell by the rigidity in his posture that Rhett's nerves were stretched tight. When the knock on the door came, she jumped. Was she about to witness a miracle or a train wreck?

Rhett led Karen to a chair on the patio while Bethany admitted Paulo. Stephanie kept Sweetness from leaping up onto the visitor. Paulo was a tall man, with dark hair and dark skin, handsome. He had that worldly, exotic look about him that Spencer worked so hard to cultivate. Paulo greeted Bethany with a polite handshake and did the same with Stephanie, avoiding the slobbering dog as best he could.

When Rhett stepped inside, Paulo's face hardened. *There is no forgiveness here*, Stephanie thought with a cold surge of dread. He ignored the hand Rhett offered.

"As I said, I did not come for you."

Bethany began to gather the dishes. Stephanie secured Sweetness to a kitchen chair and hurried to help.

Rhett cleared his throat. "Thank you for coming. I want to say that what I did to you eight years ago was wrong." The words were clear and firm, crafted over a long period of grief and regret.

Paulo's eyes flashed. "Yes, it was wrong. I loved Karen. You despised me because I was poor and from another country. You never got to know me, and yet you did your best to ruin me."

Rhett winced. "Yes. I'm sorry. I'm trying to be a better man."

Paulo cocked his head slightly, examining Rhett. "I hope that's true. You come from humble beginnings too. It was sheer hypocrisy to condemn me for that."

Rhett nodded, head bowed. "Would you like to see Karen?" he asked finally.

"Yes."

Rhett gestured him outside. Emotion flickered across Paulo's face as he stepped across the threshold and caught sight of his long-ago love. Stephanie could not resist a peek through the glass doors. She saw Karen smile when Paulo kissed her on the cheek. Rhett remained for a few minutes before he came back into the house and closed the sliding door, leaving them to talk.

Rhett's skin was pale, his mouth drawn and lines showing on his forehead. "I told him to tell her everything and anything." He sucked in a deep breath. "I am not sure how she will take it, being reminded what I did to them, but that's not important."

Bethany chewed her lip. "What is important, Rhett? What do you hope to get out of this?"

He didn't answer.

"He wants them to fall back in love again." Stephanie said. "To pick up where they left off."

"Why not?" he said, chin lifted. "God sent me on this path. Karen's life is restarting and so is mine. Why shouldn't she rediscover the love she had with Paulo if that's what God wants?"

What God wants or what you want? Seeing the fear in his eyes, Stephanie wanted to reassure him, to tell him there was every likelihood that the two would rekindle their love. But how much had changed for Paulo in these last eight years? How much had changed for Stephanie in just one day with Spencer? Would she be able to restart a relationship with him? No, but not because he'd changed, she realized. Because she had.

Stephanie Pink was not the wattleseed coffee-chasing girl anymore. She'd learned a lot about herself, particularly in the last few hundred miles. It startled her to think that maybe God had a plan for her through this journey that didn't have anything to do with that manuscript. How odd. How strange. The thought of God intervening in her life scared her. He was still not welcome in the escapades of Stephanie Pink. She shoved those thoughts away.

Rhett paced the living room, every few orbits checking on Panny nestled in a towel. Stephanie helped Bethany wash and dry the dishes, and they perked some coffee to sip, huddled in the kitchen so as not to interrupt the reunion or the pacing.

When the sliding door announced Paulo's entry into the house again, Stephanie nearly spilled her coffee.

Paulo stuck his head in the kitchen, his demeanor sad, she thought. "Thank you for having me," he said to Bethany. "It was good to see her again. Nice to meet you, Stephanie." And then he strolled out.

"Wait!" she wanted to yell. "What happened? Where do things stand?" In a moment, Sweetness pulled loose and dashed after him. Stephanie followed, snagging the leash.

Rhett was face-to-face with Paulo. "You're leaving? When will you come back?"

"We have exchanged numbers. We will keep in touch."

"That's it? That's all? Just keep in touch?" Rhett demanded.

"Yes," he said calmly. "Did you expect we would fall into each other's arms?" He laughed, a hard, bitter sound. "That's exactly what you thought, wasn't it? So naive for such an accomplished man."

Rhett's cheeks darkened. "So is this to punish me? You're rejecting Karen because you want to get back at me for what I did?"

Paulo sighed. "Your ego astounds me. Karen only has vague memories of our time together. She feels no strong connection to me, nor I to her. I have moved on. She will too. Maybe it's time you did also, Rhett." Paulo walked past him.

Rhett seized his arm. "I can help her remember. I can help you two financially."

Stephanie wanted to groan. *Oh, Rhett.*

Paulo's face went cold. "I do not want anything from you. You say you are trying to be a better man. This..." He shook his head in disgust. "This is not the actions of a man doing that."

Paulo left. Rhett stood staring out the front door. Stephanie had never felt so helpless as she did in that moment. How could she comfort Rhett? What was the way to ease the pain as he came nose to nose with his own failure?

"Rhett," she started.

He did not turn. Instead, he walked out the door and disappeared down the sidewalk.

∽

Rhett walked the neighborhood for several hours, along streets he did not know, past homes and shops he did not see. He felt alternately numb and grief stricken. Emotions clattered through him like a rusted can kicked along the gutter.

Rhett Hastings was smart, a fiscal genius, and yet his own actions seemed ludicrous and incomprehensible to him now. Had he really thought he could engineer the situation so Karen and Paulo would love each other again? Had he actually offered money to speed the deal along? The disgust in Paulo's eyes burned into Rhett, and at that moment Rhett knew that the man he had despised was his better. He'd been stupid, callous, and ridiculous.

But his plans? God's plans for him? Hadn't he been following along obediently?

"Where were You, God?" he muttered savagely, his hands balled in his pockets. "I thought this was what You wanted too." Had he been wrong about hearing God's voice? Walking away from his business? Everything? What had he done? Panic welled up inside him until he was walking so fast he was nearly running. It wasn't too late. He could get Karen settled, go back to his company, and pick up right where he left off.

He stopped at the corner, breathing hard. In his memory there was Karen, sitting in the sunlight, smiling at him, loving him the way he'd craved for so long. The very thing he'd wanted with all his heart and soul. God had given that back to him, hadn't He?

But maybe that was gone now too if Paulo had told her everything. Rhett was the brother she once again adored because she couldn't remember how he'd hurt her until Paulo came back into the picture. Paulo told her what Rhett should have said months before. He could add coward to his list of failings. How he wished he could get into his plane and fly away from his self-made disaster. His gut swirling in a wrenching tide of uncertainty, he found himself running, sprinting along the dark streets until he reached Bethany's house again.

Everything was still except for his own quickened breath. A dim light shone in the living room, and he found Karen tucked into a chair, rocking Panny as if she was a furry infant. "Stephanie showed me where the food was," she said. "We got her to eat two teaspoonfuls. Sweetness supervised until he fell asleep."

Rhett now caught sight of the big boy, lying next to Karen's chair, his legs twitching as he chased a squirrel in his dreams, the furry prize always slightly out of reach.

He sat in a chair across from her, his heart thumping. "How... how was your visit from Paulo?"

"Very nice. He remembers things much better than I do. He said we were good friends."

His heart nearly broke as he looked into her gentle blue eyes, so like his own. Anguish over the past filled him, sins that could not be undone, damage beyond repair. He couldn't go back and straighten out that wrecked past, but a tiny spark of hope still stubbornly clung to life inside him. Could there still be something good along the path that lay ahead? Did he really trust that God had a future for Rhett Hastings in spite of his disastrous choices?

He forced the words out of a mouth that had suddenly gone dry. "Karen, you were more than friends with Paulo. You loved each other. You were going to be married. I didn't think he was good enough for you, so I pulled strings and got him deported."

She stared at him in disbelief. "Paulo didn't tell me that."

"He didn't?" Rhett cleared his throat. "That's because he is a man of integrity, which is more than I can say for myself. He didn't want to tell you about the terrible thing I did because he didn't want to cause you pain."

"I'm sure you couldn't do something like that, Rhett."

Somehow he got his mouth to set the words in motion. "Yes. I could and I did. You haven't spoken to me for eight years because I hurt you so bad. You said you had no brother anymore." His throat closed up. "Karen, the head injury made you forget what a terrible brother I've been. I'm sorry. I'd give anything to undo the damage. I thought by bringing Paulo here..."

He felt tears on his cheeks. Tears. He hadn't cried since the day his mother left.

A long moment stretched between them. He could tell she was putting little bits of memory together in her mind and weighing them along with his revelation. For a moment her expression fell, and he knew she remembered enough to believe his confession.

Rhett could hardly force himself to look at her, to watch the hurt emerge again like a stubborn vine that kept springing to life after being cut away.

Oh, God, his heart cried out.

"All this..." she spread her fingers. "This plan, this arrangement to meet Paulo. It was your way of seeking atonement."

He couldn't answer.

After a moment more, she pursed her lips, reached across the dog, and took his hands in hers. He clutched her fingers.

"You didn't have to tell me the truth just now," she murmured.

"Yes, I did."

She lifted his hands to her mouth and kissed him lightly on the knuckles. "Then you're not a terrible brother anymore, are you?"

She forgave him. She saw past the sin to his boundless love for her. The forgiveness was so achingly sweet it got right inside him and filled up the places left dark for too long. He let himself cry then, and she sat with him, patting his hands and saying soothing nothings as if he was a broken-down dog left in the mud, alone and unloved. Panny reached out a tongue to lick the salty tears that fell on her thin coat.

Rhett and Karen sat for a long while together, talking some, but mostly not. When he got some control of himself, he wiped his face.

She handed him Panny and reached for her cane. "When will we leave in the morning?"

"Leave?"

"For the orchard."

The orchard. His plan had gone so completely awry, he'd thought it was all over. His plan for a reunion had fallen to splinters, but there was still the apple orchard and the spark of light that danced across Karen's face when she spoke of it. The orchard where they had spent many happy hours. A place where she could be happy in a new sort of future.

"We'll leave at ten, okay?" he managed.

He helped her stand.

Grasping her cane, she gave him a thumbs-up. "All right, big brother. I'll be ready."

Sixteen

Stephanie helped Bethany prepare breakfast. Rhett did not join them.

"Prepping the trailer," he said as he breezed through the kitchen for a cup of coffee.

She suspected he did not want to talk about the aborted reunion. She would never tell him that she'd made her way into the house to check on Panny and seen him there, sitting at his sister's side, tears flowing. Executing a quick about-face, she had returned to the trailer without being noticed.

She pondered over what she'd witnessed. Rhett had obviously told Karen the truth because Paulo had not. Paulo might not be back in Karen's life, but something had definitely happened between brother and sister, a reunion that was exactly what Rhett needed.

That could only be a God thing. Even Stephanie could not deny it. *All right, God,* she said silently. *I'll give You that one.*

She helped Karen pack a small bag, complete with several fashion magazines crammed in. Even with Sweetness in the trailer, it was cramped with three adults in the pickup, so Stephanie welcomed their occasional breaks. At every stop on the journey, she sneaked back into the trailer, trying to get her mind back to business. She intended to stalk the Jackson Agency's website, Twitter feed, and Instagram pages for any indication that they'd made contact with Agnes Wharton. Of course, they would play that close to the vest, but she knew their selfie-crazed top agent, Laura Burns, couldn't resist posting photos of herself wherever she might be, secrecy or not. One picture from Eagle Cliff, Washington, and Stephanie would know they'd stolen her author.

During their second stop, Sweetness seemed unhappy to be confined to the trailer in spite of the quick walk they'd enjoyed, but she didn't dare trust him out of her sight. He hid under the sofa, whining and sniffing, gumming his spatula, and emerging only to check on Panny.

"It's okay, Sweetness. We're on our way back to your mama. One more stop, and then it's home to Agnes."

It was a stop where they would part ways forever. Rhett had promised he would drive her to Agnes, but she could not ask him to leave Karen. She'd get a taxi or hire a driver. Then it would be a matter of miles. Sweetness delivered. Manuscript acquired. Stephanie on her way back to New York. She should be on fire for the last leg of the journey, but instead, she found herself oddly melancholy. To leave this old rusty trailer? The company of two misfit dogs? Or one flawed man who was trying so hard to become a better one?

She'd never met anyone like Rhett. So simultaneously strong and vulnerable. So arrogant and uniquely humble at the same time, a man who was bent on living out the words in his Bible, determined to climb out from beneath the shadow of his sins.

But God can use a bad man for good, can't He? He has plans to prosper us, all of us, saints, sinners, and everyone in between. She wondered if he still believed that after his plan with Paulo had fallen apart. But then she recalled the love shining on Karen's face in the lamplight. Rhett had his sister back, though not in the way he'd thought.

"Saints, sinners, and everyone in between," she said softly. "Imagine that." Thoughts of Rhett continued to whirl around in her mind until she set them firmly aside. She spent an hour surfing the Internet with no indication that Jackson's agents had made any inroads with Agnes Wharton.

Several hours later, while Rhett and Karen went in search of cold drinks at a tiny grocery store, Stephanie's phone rang. With fumbling fingers, she answered.

"This woman," Mr. Klein said without preamble. "She has called here a number of times. I gather it has something to do with your... traveling companion."

"My what? Who's been calling?"

"An Evonne somebody or other. Her diction is atrocious. Here is the number." He rattled it off and hung up.

She mulled it over. Evonne was not the "take no for an answer" type. If she didn't return her call, the woman would continue to hound Mr. Klein, who was already at the end of his patience with Stephanie. Best to face it, stonewall if necessary, and hang up quickly.

She dialed. "Hello, Evonne," she said brightly, "this is Stephanie Pink. We met in Big Thumb."

The bad connection crackled between them.

"So you finally decided to return my call," Evonne said in triumph. "You're..." More crackling. "Found you on your company website."

Stephanie was beginning to think having her name and photo plastered on a website could be a double-edged sword. "How nice. What can I do for you?"

The woman replied with something she did not catch but was most certainly not friendly small talk.

"I didn't quite hear that."

"...not going to brush me off!" Evonne snapped. Stephanie thought Mr. Klein was in error. Evonne's diction was in top form just now.

Stephanie held the phone away from her ear. "I'm not trying to brush you off. Mr. Hastings has a right to his privacy."

"He's a criminal." Intense static.

"What?" Stephanie's spine stiffened. "You don't know anything about him."

"I know enough."

Stephanie shot to her feet and began pacing. "Wise up, Evonne. You write for a newspaper, so you should know that what you read in print and online is not always the truth." Stephanie knew first-hand the power of a well-twisted word. She'd helped many a mid-list author add bows and frills to their bios.

"He's a dirty, rotten..."

Stephanie's blood was past the simmering point. "You've got no right to talk about him like that."

"I most certainly do." More crackling static.

"You listen to me, Evonne. Sure, Rhett Hastings is a ruthless businessman, and yes, a food snob. I mean, who doesn't eat white bread? And no, he doesn't say the kind and sensitive thing when he should, which I've explained makes him a blubber head, but you know what?"

"...if you'd just shut up and listen," Evonne said.

"No, you listen," Stephanie thundered in such a loud voice that Panny's head periscoped up from the blanket and Sweetness barked. "He's done a lot of bad things in his life, but he's honest about them, and he's trying to make himself better, and God is going to help him do that, which is more than I can say for most people. And besides, that darling man is nursing a dying dog back to health, and that's something they never print in the paper, now do they, Evonne?" Her voice rose to a deafening crescendo. "Now do they?"

Over her panting, she realized two things simultaneously. Her phone connection had been severed and she was shouting at no one, and Rhett stood in the doorway, his mouth open, eyes wide.

Stephanie knew her face was red. She scrolled in her mind

through the tirade he'd just overheard and fixed on two words: "Darling man." Her mortification was complete.

Rhett stood paralyzed, his eyes shifting, his mouth moving as if trying to say something, until Sweetness bounded over and bonked him on the thigh, begging to be let out of the unstable trailer and the company of an even more unstable woman.

The contact with Sweetness broke the spell, and Rhett put down the sodas he was carrying to clip the leash on Sweetness. "Uh, Karen is tired and has a bad headache. We are going to need to camp here for a while until she feels better. Is that...okay?"

Stephanie nodded. "Oh, yes. Fine. Absolutely. I was thinking about getting some more fresh air anyway. No problem."

He stood against the tugging of the eager dog. "So, uh, you don't have to defend me, you know. As a matter of fact, I don't want you tainted by my reputation."

She nodded, unable to speak. Her cheeks burning, she could only imagine what he must think of her.

He let Sweetness scoot by and scamper down the step. He went outside, and she gathered from the sounds that he had tied the dog's leash to something metallic.

She sighed, her hands pressed to her flaming cheeks as she wished the old trailer floor would open and swallow her in one gulp. She was startled when he came back in.

"But...that was nice, what you said." His mouth quirked in a smile.

One curl tumbled over his forehead as he stood there contemplating her. She wanted to reach out and tuck it back into place, to feel the springy coil against her fingers. What an imperfect, arrogant, earnest, darling man. Darling man. Oh, there it was again, the pesky thought.

She shrugged. "You're right. You don't need me to defend you."

He took her hand and pulled her to him. His arms circled her waist, and he embraced her, his head pressed close, his body warm and strong next to hers.

He pressed a soft kiss to the corner of her mouth, sending tingles up and down her spine, and brushed her neck with his lips. "But it's nice to have someone see the good things."

He lingered there a moment, and she realized she was not breathing. Then he let her go and hastened back outside to Sweetness.

She stood in shock. He'd probably meant it to be a friendly kiss, but he had no idea how it had awakened such a powerful feeling of longing that she was immobilized by it. Never with Spencer or any other man had she felt such a connection.

She shook herself, in much the same way she'd seen Sweetness do a number of times. "Listen up, Pink," she scolded. "You've got a job to do, so do it. This guy's going to go off and be an apple wrangler or some such thing, and you two are just friends. Remember the wedding cake."

She intoned it with the same graveness as "remember the Alamo." Love meant loss and self-loathing and frosting smashed into tire treads. "Remember your goals."

Soon-to-be agent Stephanie Pink marched to the sofa, scooped up Panny, and plunged outside without further delay.

∽

Rhett made sure Karen ate half of one of Stephanie's bologna and cheese sandwiches (this time she'd added pickles to up the gourmet factor) and helped her upstairs to the little bedroom.

"Why don't you sleep on the sofa?" he'd asked her. "That's a lot of stairs to navigate."

"Rhett," she said, fixing him with an icy glare that reminded him of how she'd reacted upon hearing he'd been expelled from high school. "Stop babying me. If I'm going to run an apple orchard, I'm going to have to get my strength back. So go count some money or something and let me be."

He grinned as he returned downstairs, relishing his sister's admonishment. Stephanie hunched over her phone, staring at the screen, a finger tapping impatiently on the kitchen table. The front door was open to let in the afternoon sun, and a scent of pine wafted through the air.

"Karen just needs an hour or two, tops." He checked his watch. "Then we'll be back on the road again. We can be at the orchard around midnight, barring any unforeseen complications."

"Sounds great."

He wasn't sure how to proceed. The kiss he'd given her after hearing her stalwart defense of him still tingled on his mouth. And he thought he'd felt a response in her, that she welcomed the kiss, but he had to be wrong about that. He was a convenient means to an end for her, a way to speed her and the ungainly Sweetness along to their destination. Business. Keep it all business.

Panny eyed him from her place on the sofa. She appeared to be holding her head up better now, but her food intake was still minimal, and she had yet to show signs of trying to walk.

He'd purchased a thirty-foot leash with which to secure Sweetness so the dog could have a chance to explore around the trailer without wandering off again. Currently, Sweetness was snuffling through the bushes outside, peeing and sniffing in happy canine fashion. *That dog has personality plus,* Rhett thought. He was going to miss the big guy when Stephanie finally returned him to his rightful owner.

He pulled out some supplies from the fridge and felt Stephanie watching him.

She raised an eyebrow. "Didn't get enough bologna and cheese?"

"I figured I'd put together some dinner for later." He fetched onions and butter.

"What's it going to be?"

"Soupe à l'oignon."

"Sounds fancy."

"Just French onion soup. I'm going to use canned broth, so it won't be as good as if I used homemade."

He caught the eye roll. "You know there's nothing wrong with taking the time to cook up something properly with fresh ingredients and all."

"Are you implying there's something substandard about raviolis from a can and bologna on white bread?" Her eyes were teasing, dancing with fun. He resisted the urge to scoop her into his arms and pick up where he'd left off.

"Not at all. So far, we are still alive."

She laughed just before her attention was drawn to her phone.

"Oh, no!" Stephanie gasped, peering at the screen.

"What?"

She turned the phone around to show him the selfie of a plump woman wearing some sort of odd cloche hat, standing at an airport Starbuck's.

"It's Laura." Stephanie's face was grave.

"She's a problem?"

"An agent for our rivals. She's getting on a plane to fly to California."

He got it. "Uh-oh. Is this the competition rolling into town?"

"Yes." She bit her lip. "She's trying to get to Agnes before I do."

He wondered for a split second how Stephanie's life might change if Laura beat her to the prize, but her stricken look put him into problem-solving mode.

"Take a selfie. Caption it 'Preparing for the biggest meeting of my life.' Laura will see that you've snagged the deal and she won't bother."

"Do you think so?"

Rhett tossed an onion into the air and caught it. "Trust me. I'm a baron in the boardroom. Isn't that what Google says about me?"

"It also says you're a corporate thug."

He laughed. "You can't believe everything you read on Google."

She took the selfie. "Okay. Now one with you."

He tried to wave her away with the spoon. "Camera shy."

"Uh-uh. I promise it won't go up on social media. It's just for me to remember."

His heart squeezed as he held his face close to hers.

To remember.

When I'm gone.

He breathed in the sweet scent of her, pressed his rough cheek next to her satin one, and forced himself to smile.

Seventeen

Stephanie whiled away an hour taking Sweetness for a walk while Rhett unhitched the truck and drove off in search of a store to buy a new cushion for Panny, whom Rhett had decided needed accommodations finer than the bath towel they'd been using.

Rhett's mother hen tendencies made her smile. Agnes Wharton had seen the same tender streak in her love, Jedd, when he'd happened on a baby rabbit just after the mother had been snatched away by a hawk. Stephanie had read the passage so many times she could recite it from memory.

The tiny thing in Jedd's calloused hands wriggled, blind and weak. His hard face, softened and gentled by the helplessness of it, stirred something inside me, something both angry and mournful. How could there be tenderness in him for this ragged creature when all of the gentle places in my soul had been lacquered over by the loss of our baby? How could he still show love to an animal when we could hardly look at each other past the aching void? Yet he did, and in that moment I knew I could still love him too.

Moisture pricked Stephanie's eyes, and she braced herself against it. What madness was sending these wild emotions firing through her when the clock was ticking? Laura was on the hunt, and if Stephanie's selfie ruse didn't work, her chance at the manuscript was in jeopardy.

They were back to the trailer now, and Sweetness cocked a floppy ear in the direction of the open upstairs window. He let out a low whine. Stephanie had to listen harder until she heard a slight sniffling sound from Karen's room.

Crying. She was uncertain what to do. She did not know Karen well, and though she was much better than Rhett at recognizing what compassion should sound like, she was not at all sure she was in the Mrs. Granato category of sympathetic listeners. The sniffling continued, along with a whimper. *Do something, Steph.* But what should she say? She had no idea. *Saints and sinners,* she thought suddenly. Rhett said God used both, and since there were no saintly Mrs. Granatos around at the moment, the seriously flawed Stephanie Pink would have to do.

After a deep breath, she opened the trailer door, and Sweetness pranced impatiently until she unhooked his leash. Then he was up the stairs before she could say a word.

The scrambling of his paws on the wood was followed by a loud exclamation. Stephanie raced up, fearing the dog had knocked Karen to the floor. She found her on her back on the bed with Sweetness standing over her, swabbing her face with his tongue as she batted weakly at him.

"Oh, you bad dog," Stephanie said, hauling him to the floor. He barked and hopped, pleased with himself and ready to accept what he surely thought must be praise. "Sit!" she commanded. Instead, he dove under the bed and reappeared with his spatula. Sprawling on the floor, he sat down to fuss over it.

Karen sat up and wiped her face with the back of her hand. "Weird dog."

"I concur." Stephanie shifted. "He, uh, heard some crying. Are you okay?"

Karen pushed a clump of hair from her face. "Oh, I was just leafing through these fashion magazines. They brought back some memories." She gestured to her worn jeans and faded T-shirt. "You'd never guess it, but I use to have some nice things. Paulo planned to take me to Lima someday and show me off." She sighed and rubbed her hands along her thin legs. "Not much to show off anymore."

Stephanie sank down onto the bed next to her. "So you...do remember? About Paulo?"

She nodded. "It's been coming back to me more and more. I didn't tell Rhett. It's better for him to think I just don't remember much about the two of us." She sniffled. "I really loved Paulo. I guess I still do. He stopped loving me, of course. Eight years will do that." Her face crumpled. "We were going to be married."

"I'm sorry," was all Stephanie could think of to say. Images of the little tissue paper bells she'd purchased for her own wedding flashed before her eyes. "I had a false start wedding too."

"Yeah? Did you break it off or did he?"

"He did, but I...er...reacted badly. It's funny, but the whole time I was running over the wedding cake, I just kept thinking about my mother. She'd been so happy to think of me getting married. It was the only time I'd seen her happy since my brother died. She bought us a cake knife. I still have it somewhere because it has our names engraved on it—Spencer and Stephanie. My mother beamed when she gave it to us at the bridal shower. It crushed her when the plans changed. I have massive guilt about that." Stephanie blushed. "I don't know why I'm telling you all this."

Karen touched Stephanie's arm. "It's all this talk of weddings. Paulo and I were going to buy a little farm and work it together as soon as he got his paperwork in order. That's why he was employed when he shouldn't have been. He was trying to save money so we could fly home and meet his family."

Stephanie thought of Rhett with all his millions and the proud Paulo scraping together every dime. Both men who had loved and wanted the best for Karen.

"Rhett thought Paulo was after me as a way to stay in the States, that he was really after the Hastings fortune." She shook her head. "I never wanted any part of Rhett's money and neither did Paulo. He didn't used to be that way, you know? Rhett, I mean. He was fourteen when my mom left. It changed him, hardened something here." She patted her chest.

"She didn't stay in contact with you both?"

"She tried, on and off, but Rhett and my dad were so hostile, she eventually stopped coming until it was too late."

"She died?"

"No, she runs a bead shop in San Francisco. She's not a bad person, just weak. She had the biological components to be a mother, but not the courage. I visit her sometimes, but I never tell Rhett because it would make him furious. You know the saddest thing?" She rubbed her nose. "He knows all about the bead shop because he looked up her Facebook page. I saw it on his computer once. So sad. He would never admit it, but he wants his mom back. Maybe God will make that happen someday."

Stephanie picked up one of the magazines that had fallen to the floor. Karen had dog-eared a page. "Silk?" she said, pointing to the elegant scarf worn by an impossibly thin model.

"Yes. Lovely, isn't it? Paulo always said the people in Lima would stop dead in their tracks when they saw me strolling along. I guess I don't really need a scarf like that anymore, do I? A middle-aged woman with brain damage and a ruined body?" Tears sparkled again and Stephanie took her hand. "At least I know what love felt like. Memories count for something, don't they?"

What could she say that would ease the pain? She squeezed Karen's fingers. Stephanie's loss had been different, and somehow the same.

"It's funny, in a way," Karen said. "We had a plan, Paulo and me, but Rhett couldn't accept it. He had his own plan, which didn't work out either." She sighed. "But Paulo is happy, and I've got my brother back, and Rhett...well, he's finally found the Lord, so I guess God's plan trumped all of ours, didn't it?"

Except for the pain part. Stephanie shifted. "I don't trust God's plans," she mumbled. "Not since Ian died."

"Rhett told me you had a brother," she said gently. "I'm sorry you lost him."

"Me too. He was one of those people who never said a bad thing about anyone. He was like sunshine in a bottle, my mother used to say."

"And you're carrying the bottle for him now?"

She stared. "What do you mean?"

"Rhett said you're going to work out a plan to be a literary agent, like Ian wanted."

She detached herself from Karen's grasp, embarrassed that Rhett had seen fit to share with his sister all about Stephanie's misguided plans. "We both wanted it. Rhett doesn't understand that."

"And you want it still?"

"What?"

"The life you imagined before."

Anger flashed through her. What right did these messed-up siblings have to cast doubt on her motivations? "What I really want is my brother back," she said, horrified when the words spilled out and tears started in her eyes. "Like you want what you had with Paulo. But I'm not going to get it and neither are you." Immediately she closed her eyes. "I'm sorry."

"It's okay." Karen sighed, low and soft. "When our mom left, Rhett was filled with rage. He felt unimportant and insignificant, and he made it the mission of his life to prove he wasn't. The constant fighting at school, the lies, his business dealings—they were all to plug the hole left by my mom. My dad was a hard man, and he

couldn't show love. He just wasn't wired that way. He was tough on
Rhett, way too tough. I prayed and prayed that God's love would
fill up that empty space inside my brother. And it did, finally, but it
was a long journey for both of us."

Stephanie stood, desperately wanting to leave. "I've had a long
journey too, and I'm getting close to the finish line. As a matter of
fact, I'd better send a few e-mails before—" she stopped abruptly,
hearing the crunch of wheels outside. "Great. Rhett's back. Time
to take off again."

Karen still watched her in that way that made her squirm. Sweetness continued to mangle his spatula. The room seemed very small.
How had she allowed her plans to get so far off track? Her gut tightened, breathing shallowed. Her plans, her goals, her life. *Butt out,
Karen. And you too, Rhett.*

Karen spoke softly as Stephanie headed for the stairs. "The hard
part isn't losing someone. It's learning who you are without them."

I know who I am, Stephanie thought. Stepping onto stairs that
felt wobbly, in a trailer that she had despised only days before, she
tried to picture herself as she had been, wearing her smart suit, ready
to seal a deal, confident of her plan. She'd been in charge, Stephanie Pink, sure of herself.

And then there was Sweetness.

And Rhett.

Distractions, delays.

The descriptors rang hollow. They were something more.

She pushed the discomfort aside.

Time to take off.

∽

Rhett took a calming breath and explained for the third time.
"There's a wreck about three miles up the road. A truck with a load
of bricks turned over at the freeway junction, and it's going to take

them a few hours to clear the on-ramp. We might as well have dinner and then head out." He took the spoon from her hand and sprinkled the flour over the onions he'd caramelized earlier. "Don't dump in the flour. Stir it in gently."

She huffed. "Maybe they've cleared it. You should go check."

"I have a road conditions app on my phone. It's still not passable." He opened the cans of broth. If only he'd had enough time to make it from scratch.

"We could go another way."

"Yes, but that would take more than an hour so we wouldn't be gaining any time."

"At least we'd be moving," she grumped. She poked her head outside to check on Sweetness, who was once again foraging in the bushes, tethered to his long leash.

The frown lingered on Stephanie's face as she returned to the stove. He understood. So close to her goal, like a runner stopped a few yards from the victory tape. It made sense, but it saddened him anyway. So anxious to leave? *No, anxious to succeed,* he chided himself. Don't make it personal. "No updates from Laura?"

"Nope. It's driving me crazy. Mr. Klein has stopped e-mailing me, which is also driving me nuts."

"Maybe you should deal with Mr. Gregory."

She sighed. "There is no Mr. Gregory. When Mr. Klein started the agency, he thought it would add to the allure if there were two agents employed there."

"So he made up a partner?"

"Yes. Nowadays we just tell people who ask that Mr. Gregory is semiretired."

"Book people are weird."

"So true."

He handed her a wooden spoon. "Stir while I pour in the broth."

She started off in vigorous swipes.

"Stir, not brutalize," he commanded.

"You are bossy."

"And you are a wreck in the kitchen."

She pointed a finger at him. "That was unkind, and wreck is way overstated. I know my way around a slice of bologna, don't I?"

He was going to add a sarcastic remark, but something about the soft bow of her mouth and the delicately arched eyebrow stopped him. "I apologize," he said simply. "Thank you for helping."

She relaxed a fraction. "It smells good."

"Yes, it does. In an hour, we'll be enjoying a delicious soup complete with a floating island of cheese toast."

She let loose with a peal of laughter that both thrilled and irked him. "Floating cheese toast? Who taught you how to cook, anyway?"

"I taught myself." A long-buried memory bubbled to the surface. "I used to sneak into cinemas when I was a kid, and the theater manager in the small town where we lived cooked on a hot plate in the back room after hours. He made ragout and stroganoff and all kinds of things I'd never heard of." It was, in fact, the best food he'd ever tasted. His cheeks burned when he recalled that he had snuck into that back room and sampled the food like some sort of vagabond. She didn't need to know that part. "It smelled so good it made me want to learn how to cook too."

He would not tell her either that he'd proudly tried out a recipe for beef ragout for his family, the ingredients purchased out of his meager wages. His dad had sniffed dubiously and pronounced it "fancified slop" and fixed a sandwich instead. Rhett could still hear the sound of the knife on the plate as he'd scraped the food into the trash.

"He didn't mean it," Karen had whispered.

Yes, he had.

He shook himself back to the present. "I had this crazy notion that theaters should sell more than popcorn and candy. We now have a dozen theaters across the country that serve everything from salmon sliders to lobster rolls."

"So I guess you don't get many poor folks in your theaters."

He stopped stirring. "On Wednesdays, all movies are a buck. Everywhere, in every state, in every one of my theaters without exception. I remember what it felt like to be a kid without enough for a ticket. I'm not the heartless monster I'm made out to be in the press." He thought of Paulo. "Not completely, anyway."

She touched his arm, her beautiful eyes catching his, drawing him in if he let them. Her fingers grazed his wrist, exciting his pulse.

"I'm sorry," she said. "Now I'm the one being insensitive."

He shrugged. "Anyway, after dinner, the on-ramp should be cleared and off we go, full speed ahead. We'll bunk for the night at the orchard, and by the end of the weekend you will have that manuscript in your possession." He forced a happy tone. *Finish line, remember, Rhett? You knew this was the deal.*

Karen came downstairs. "Why did you let me sleep so long?"

"Because you're going to have to read the map for the next part. The GPS isn't going to help find the orchard."

"What smells so good?"

"French onion soup with cheesy toast islands," Stephanie said promptly.

Karen laughed. "My brother is still the gourmand, I see. That hasn't changed. I would have been just fine with peanut butter and jelly."

"French onion soup is better than peanut butter and jelly. That's not snobbery. It's a universal truth." He lowered the heat to simmer on the soup and went for the Gruyère in the fridge while Karen settled herself cross-legged on the rocking chair with Panny in her lap.

Rhett stuck his head in a cupboard. "Did you see a cheese grater around here, or did Sweetness get hold of that too?"

"I don't..." Stephanie's words were drowned out by a sound unlike anything Rhett had ever heard before.

Eighteen

This time it was not a feeble, geriatric dog Sweetness had decided to save. As he lugged the gyrating animal inside, Stephanie leaped onto the bench seat, followed by Rhett right next to her. The hissing cat, lanky and striped, contorted wildly, striking at Sweetness on the face and ears. Undeterred, Sweetness held firmly onto the cat's scruff, presenting the ferocious thing for inspection.

From the dim recesses of her mind, Stephanie understood this was not some domesticated tabby but a feral cat. It was probably a good twelve pounds, strong and agile, and not at all used to being manhandled by a Good Samaritan dog. Puffs of fur volleyed through the air.

"Sweetness!" Rhett bellowed. "Drop it!"

Sweetness cocked his head as he considered, sending the cat off kilter, whereupon it unleashed a new round of frantic slashing. A pinwheeling claw caught Sweetness on the ear, and he whined but did not loosen his grip.

Karen clutched Panny close. "He's going to get cut to ribbons."

"Drop that cat!" Rhett thundered again.

Sweetness looked from Rhett to Stephanie, the movement jog-gling the cat back and forth. The cat let loose with a bloodcur-dling yowl. Sweetness finally complied and opened his mouth. The enraged cat landed feet first on the tile. The feline ears were flat-tened, its mouth wide, showing neat rows of needle-like teeth, limbs stretched, every muscle and sinew taut.

"Still a cat lover?" Rhett said from the corner of his mouth.

"I'm not sure that's really a cat," she whispered back.

The enraged animal arched its back and let out a noise that was more akin to a human shriek than a meow, its claws slicing in a full-out assault as it sprang. The dog dove under the kitchen table, wedg-ing himself there until only his shivering rump was exposed. The cat set to work, clawing and biting at the canine behind. Piteous whim-pers came from under the kitchen table.

"Oh, no!" Karen cried. "Rhett! You have to do something."

"What? All I've got is a cheese grater." He waved the instrument helplessly.

"Bad cat! Bad, bad, cat!" Stephanie yelled.

"I don't think that's going to do the trick." Rhett handed her the grater, leaped off the bench seat, grabbed the broom, and gave the cat a swat. The cat whirled to face the new attacker.

As Stephanie held her breath, the cat's eyes glowed with molten anger. It pounced on the broom, latching onto the bristles with a vicious bite.

"Be careful," Stephanie called. "It might have diseases."

Rhett pulled the connected broom and cat in an effort to get the animal closer to the door. Instead, it let go and leaped onto the kitchen counter. "Get away from my soup!" he yelled.

"Let it have the soup." Stephanie stepped carefully off the seat.

Rhett's eyes flashed. "There is no way this cat is going to ruin my French onion soup." Using the pot lid as a shield against the slashing claws, he maneuvered the cat away from the stove, edging it slowly toward the door.

Stephanie snatched up the bench seat cushion and approached from the other side to be sure the cat didn't head back into the kitchen. Slowly, with much hissing and swiping, the animal was eased toward the exit. With one final look of disgust beamed at the trailer occupants, the cat streaked out the door and down the steps, disappearing once again into the bushes.

Rhett heaved out a sigh of relief and wiped the sweat from his brow. Stephanie lowered the sofa cushion. It took her a moment to realize the miracle that was taking place behind her. Sweetness was still stuffed under the table, quivering and whining, but little Panny was standing up on Karen's lap, barking vigorously in a volume just north of a whisper.

Karen watched her, face lit up in an exact match of Rhett's. "Well, look who's come to join the party."

Rhett hurried over, kneeling down next to the minuscule dog. "Panny," he said, stroking the dog's quivering ears. "Look at you. You're standing up."

The wonder on his face almost made Stephanie cry. Panny stopped barking and gave Rhett a lick on his chin. "Good job, girl. You scared that nasty cat away, didn't you?"

Panny absorbed the praise and gave one more raspy bark before she settled back down on Karen's lap to finish her nap.

"You see?" Rhett said triumphantly. "I told you she would get better."

His exuberance lit his entire face, lifted his shoulders, and made him appear every bit a victorious lion. Stephanie laughed and kissed him on the cheek. "Bravo, Rhett. I guess it was all your doctoring that did it."

He grinned, retrieving the grater from where she'd laid it. "And maybe a little added motivation from a feral cat."

"I'm still not sure that was a cat," Stephanie said. "It was more like a small, hostile tiger."

"Sweetness would agree with you on that point." They both

looked at the still-shivering bottom protruding from under the table. "Can you try your hand at some first aid for the big lug while I finish up the soup?"

"I don't think I'm qualified," Stephanie said. "I'm not a dog person, remember?"

"Time to rewrite your résumé," he said, saluting her with the cheese grater.

⁂

The soup filled the trailer with a sumptuous aroma that made Stephanie's mouth water. Rhett fussed around with his cheese islands, and Karen held Sweetness still while Stephanie cleaned and applied some antibacterial spray to the dog's bitten behind.

"Good thing you have plenty of fur down here," Stephanie said. "Only one little nick and that scratch on your ear. That should teach you to be more selective about the company you bring home."

Sweetness was so dejected, he would do no more than slink back under the table. Karen set Panny down nearby, and the two cuddled close. When the bowls of onion soup complete with cheesy toast islands were handed round, Stephanie thought she had never enjoyed such a special meal in her whole life. Karen and Rhett seemed to feel the same, contentment written all over their faces.

Rhett joined hands with his sister and Stephanie. He said a simple grace, his fingers warm and gentle in hers. "All that we have, is a gift. It comes, O God, from You. Thank You."

After the "amen," Stephanie smiled at him. "You googled some more prayers?"

"I thought that one captured the big points, even though it doesn't rhyme."

They ate the soup, and it was, as Stephanie expected, the most incredible thing she had ever had the privilege to consume. Was it the savory beef broth or the way the cheese melted into unctuous ribbons that mingled with the onions? Perhaps it was the bits of bread, silky and luxurious on her tongue.

As she looked around, the sunset painting the sky outside the trailer windows, she suspected that the soup was seasoned with ingredients far more precious and rare.

Two nutty dogs, snuggling together to comfort one another.

A sister who had lost a love and found her brother.

A trailer held together with duct tape and memories.

And a man who knew how to make islands out of cheese.

It comes, O God, from You.

Her own sense of gratitude in that moment did not surprise her as much as it would have a week before.

She imagined it would not have surprised Mrs. Granato either.

∽

Rhett whistled a tune as he guided the truck and trailer along the highway with Karen crammed between him and Stephanie. The darkness crept in, and Karen used a flashlight to check the map more and more frequently as the hours went by. The terrain became decidedly rural as they left the highway. When they stopped so that Stephanie could take the dogs out for a potty break, he rolled down his window and breathed in the scent of dry grass. Rhett wondered if Stephanie had noticed the same things he had as they drove along—the heavy canopy of trees, the chitter of crickets, and the small roadside fruit stands, shuttered until morning. But she had not, he decided. She was probably focused on the whereabouts of literary agent Laura.

"You're thinking of Stephanie, aren't you?"

He blinked at his sister. "What? No. Why would you say that?"

She gave him the same maddening smile she'd doled out repeatedly when they were teens. "What's this?" She tapped the tattered paperback he'd stuck under the driver's side visor. "*Red Lady Lost*," she read from the title.

"Some detective novel I picked up."

"I didn't know you'd become a fiction lover."

"I got it for Stephanie," he admitted. "She has to have books around all the time for some reason. She gets antsy without something to read."

"I see," she said in a tone he didn't care for.

He glared. "Don't get any ideas. She's only along for the ride."

"If you say so."

He did want to say so, though he figured trying to explain it to Karen would only make him look foolish. What had tripped his sister's matchmaker radar? Had he given some sort of signal that Stephanie was occupying too much of his thoughts? He resolved to watch for signs of that tendency and squash them as Stephanie and Panny rejoined them. She reported that Sweetness was settled inside the trailer with his spatula.

The rode became bumpier still when they came within the last few miles of their destination. Potholes dotted the asphalt as they passed the little town where they had spent time as children.

"Sparrowville has changed," Karen said, peering out into the night. "Where did the ice-cream shop go? And the bowling alley is all boarded up."

He noted that many of the storefronts appeared to be empty. The buildings, caught in the sickly glow of streetlights, were old and weathered, and the few cars parked along the street were no better. A gas station sign blinked a forlorn Morse code. Perhaps it was the darkness that gave the town the sheen of desolation.

"Economy's been tough on small towns. It will probably look better in the morning," he said, though it troubled him.

Karen didn't answer. He rumbled through town and searched for the narrow road that would lead up to Dappled Acres. Another surge of nostalgia hit him with surprising force. During many a sleepless night he thought he would never again clap eyes on this orchard and the aged farmhouse, especially after it was sold years before when his grandfather died. His shock at finding out it was for sale again still echoed inside him. A God thing. It could be nothing else. He'd called the real estate agent, who'd eagerly sent him pictures, and delivered the full asking price in cash that same day, sight unseen. Not a smart way to do business, not Rhett's way, but he'd done it nonetheless.

And now they were here. It was surreal. The long sloping road up to the ranch was as he remembered it, though the trees had grown to massive heights and crowded together along the roadside. He'd have a crew in to cut them back before the storm season arrived.

There was only a sliver of moon and the headlights to guide them. The tires picked up rocks that pinged and rang against the sides of the truck, which caused Panny to sit up.

Karen's face was eager, her body straining forward. She pointed to a crooked sign. "Dappled Acres Apple Orchard. I can't believe it."

He felt all the weight of the world slip away. He'd done it. In spite of all the damage, he'd brought her home. And she'd let him. His soul expanded with a gratefulness that was almost too big to contain.

"It's like a dream to be back here, Rhett."

Too emotional to risk a response, he nodded and kept the truck rumbling steadily upward. Another mile and the road flattened out somewhat. To his left was a heavy screen of trees. To the right, the old barn, with a sunken roof.

"Going to have to replace that," Rhett said. Karen didn't seem to hear.

She peered ahead into the night. "That's new."

He braked to a stop at an iron gate. "Never had a gate in Grandpa's day." Well, they had to expect a few things had changed in the many years since they'd been there. He got out and went to open it, but he found a heavy padlock in place, for which he had no key.

Irritated, he took out his cell and dialed the real estate agent's number, ready to let him have it despite the time, which was after midnight. The phone rang and rang with no answer. No voicemail either? Odd, but perhaps not so unusual for a small-town Realtor.

He stabbed the "end call" button and yanked on the lock again. It was solid and unyielding, and he fought the urge to aim a hearty kick at the metal rails.

Karen joined him, walking stiffly. She held a hand to her back as if to quell a pain. Lines of fatigue aged her.

Stephanie walked up, carrying Panny. She also had Sweetness on his leash. He didn't seem to be slowed by his injured rump. "What's up?" she asked with a yawn. "This is the place, right?"

"Gate's locked. I don't have a key." He looked beyond the fence. "It's another two miles to the farmhouse. I'll climb the fence and see if I can locate a key or some bolt cutters or something. You two stay here."

"Leave it until morning," Karen said. "Let's sleep in the trailer. I'm tired, and you shouldn't go traipsing around in the dark."

"I—"

But she was already making her way back to the truck.

"She's right, Rhett," Stephanie said. "No sense walking in the dark and risking falling into a pit or encountering an angry bear or something."

He raised an eyebrow. "Too many adventure novels."

"Probably, but Karen's tired, and she's not going to rest if you're out there making like Grizzly Adams."

He didn't answer, leaning his elbows against the gate and peering out into the darkness.

"What's wrong?" she said.

He wasn't sure. "Do you smell smoke?"

She sniffed. "Not smoke, exactly. More like the lingering smell of the kitchen after you burn a bag of microwave popcorn. You know how the odor sticks around for a long time?" She raised an eyebrow. "Let me guess. You've never had microwave popcorn."

"I'm a movie theater guy. If I can't see it tumble out of the popper, it isn't worth eating."

"With a side of truffle oil, I'm sure."

He laughed, and it lightened his unaccounted-for anxiety. "I guess you'll have to add popcorn snob to my list of sins."

"Duly noted."

Her nearness drew the words out of him. "It's funny. This is the moment I've waited and planned for, and now that it's here I can't shake the feeling that something is about to go completely wrong."

Her face was thoughtful in the moonlight, perfect arcs and planes, a masterpiece. He swallowed.

"You know, Rhett, one thing I'm learning on this trip is that just because things don't go according to plan, that doesn't mean they're turning out wrong."

There was something tender in her glance. Was she actually happy that Sweetness had made the mad dash in Big Thumb? That she'd wound up with a mixed-up mogul in his busted-down trailer? He couldn't be sure. He wouldn't dare think it. He shoved his hands in his pockets and looked again at the darkened landscape.

"Let's deal with this in the morning," she said. "Come on, Sweetness."

But the dog would not come, not until Rhett made his way along also. When Rhett flopped down onto the worn sofa, Sweetness offered a slurping good night kiss and trotted off to find Panny, who Rhett figured had snuggled up next to Karen. The floor creaked as Karen and Stephanie settled themselves for the night, and then the trailer subsided into stillness. Outside, the crickets practiced their symphony, and he almost forgot about the faint scent of something long burned that still hung heavy in his senses.

Nineteen

Stephanie woke when she heard the rumble of an approaching vehicle. She pulled on some clothes and scrambled to the tiny window as a dusty blue pickup parked next to Rhett's. The sun was working its way into an upright position, though it was not yet six a.m.

Karen emerged with Panny, excitement on her face. "I can't wait for you to see Dappled Acres, Stephanie."

She found that her own stomach was tingling with excitement as she followed Karen downstairs. Rhett was already up and out, so the women exited the trailer quickly. The air was cool, thick with the scent of morning dew on grass and that lingering aroma of something scorched.

Rhett and a skinny bearded man in jeans and a worn denim jacket stood together. Sweetness broke off his examination of the man to greet Stephanie, Karen, and Panny.

"Morning," the man said, extending a hand. "Jack Wershing from over the hill. Brought this gate key over. Mr. Phipps gave it to me after he sold you the place. Figured you'd be along soon enough to collect it. Norm in town told me he'd seen you head up here with your trailer last night."

Rhett frowned. "I don't understand why Mr. Phipps didn't hand the key over to me directly."

Jack rubbed his face. "Dunno. I don't go into town much. He has a shop in Fallsbury if you want to go ask him. It's about fifty miles from here." He eyed Rhett. "You gonna put up a bed-and-breakfast or something? Build a vacation home?"

"No," Karen beamed a brilliant smile on him. "This used to be our family orchard. We're going to take it over and run it."

Confusion flickered across his weathered face. "Yeah? Well, that's fine then. I've got to go, but here's my cell number. Call if you need anything." He handed over a scrap of paper that Stephanie took because Rhett was already unlocking the gate.

Jack drove quickly away, puffs of dust rising up from under his tires.

"He looked surprised about something," Stephanie mused, but Rhett wasn't listening. He'd swung wide the gate and hastened to the truck. Stephanie put Sweetness back inside the trailer, and then she joined Karen and Panny in the pickup. Rhett drove toward a farmhouse visible in the distance.

The property was backed on one side by a series of high hills. Set into a bowl of a valley were acres and acres of trees.

It's so dark, she thought. *Like the scary* Wizard of Oz *trees.* She'd had something much lighter and brighter in mind. The closer they came, the more confused she got. When they jerked to a stop near a grimy, ranch-style house, Rhett exploded from the truck like a launched missile. Stephanie got out on her side a little more slowly and then went to open the trailer door for Sweetness.

What she saw was right out of an apocalyptic novel. Behind the farmhouse, the trees were dead and scorched, twisted branches like claws against the rising sun. Rows and rows of incinerated apple trees stood in tidy rank and file. It was what she imagined a nuclear winter would look like.

Karen stared.

Rhett approached the house. Finding the front door locked, he hastened to the rear. Stephanie followed, stopping short as Rhett let loose with a stream of ire. The back of the structure was just as blackened as the trees, where the flames must have licked up against the walls before they'd been extinguished. The wood was blistered and peeled back, and missing pieces of glass jigsawed the ruined windows.

Karen shuffled around to join them, leaning on her cane. Her expression was shocked, grief stricken. Stephanie moved closer and took possession of Panny because Karen seemed to have lost the strength to hold the dog properly.

"I'm so sorry," Stephanie said.

Karen shook her head. "From the front, you'd never guess."

"No." She groped for something to say but came up with nothing.

Rhett approached the broken sliding door that hung crooked on its track. A white ball of fluff streaked by, followed by another. The two chickens squawked and fussed as they trotted past a startled Sweetness.

He barked and lunged, retreated and lunged again, and then he turned around in a circle, quivering all over in comic indecision.

"Good restraint, dog. Remember the cat incident," Stephanie advised.

Sweetness decided to stalk the birds from a safe distance, hanging back several feet as the fowl set about pecking for bugs in a patch of unscorched grass next to the porch steps.

Rhett emerged from the house. "It's ruined. Unlivable. The electrical and water are still working, but the place reeks of smoke, and the wild animals have been making themselves at home inside."

He moved quickly past them and headed to the trees, his feet crunching on the grass. Stephanie followed uncertainly. Here and there blades of green poked through the black, indicating some time had passed since the fire. She felt a spark of hope. Did apple trees come back to life as quickly as the grass? She hadn't the foggiest notion. It was all she could do to keep her ficus alive.

Rhett made his way to the nearest tree branch and put out a hand to test the wood. To Stephanie's horror, a ten-inch section broke off with all the finality of a limb being amputated. The sound of the hollow snap lingered. Her stomach twisted.

He stood there, holding the ruined branch, his fingers stained black with soot, staring at the dead thing in his fist.

"He sold me a ruined orchard."

"Is it really ruined?" she asked, stepping closer. "Could there be—"

He cut her off. "Mr. Phipps sent me pictures, very carefully staged pictures, and because I wanted the property, I didn't look too hard. He cheated me, and I let him."

"What are you going to do?"

His voice was flat, emotionless, and terrifying as he hurled the ruined branch away. "Would you stay here with Karen for a couple hours? I need to go to Fallsbury. You can stay in the trailer."

"Uh, do you want me to come with you?"

He didn't answer as he turned and walked rapidly toward the truck.

"Rhett..."

He didn't slow.

"Remember, you're a better man," she wanted to say.

Not a corporate thug, but a man who saves old dogs.

And gives rides to desperate literary agent assistants.

A guy who's following God.

"You're a good man, Rhett Hastings," she said instead.

But he'd already unhooked the trailer, gunned the engine, and was hurtling down the road.

ᥫᩣ

Rhett drove to Fallsbury, waves of alternating rage and disbelief coursing through him. He was not even aware of the roads he'd taken or the turns he'd managed as he arrived at the Fallsbury Real Estate Office.

He parked illegally, marched up to the door, and tried to shove it open.

Locked.

He rattled the door handle several times, and then he checked his watch. It was only seven thirty. Of course they wouldn't be open. Then he noticed the pile of newspapers littering the entryway. An "Out of Business" sign was written in marker and taped to the window.

Out of Business. Sweat broke out on his forehead.

A woman walking an overweight Labrador stopped. "Phipps closed up his shop two weeks ago."

"Did he say where he was going?"

She laughed. "Always talked about living on a boat in the Florida Keys. Business has been real slow, so he probably figured it would be just the time to get out while the getting is good."

Yeah, after he'd made a killing off some naive chump, namely R. Hastings. Rhett feared his heart was about to jump out of his chest.

She peered at him. "Aren't you that guy..."

He restrained a groan. Why did his picture have to be plastered on every news forum and gossip rag? The great Rhett Hastings, a Fortune 500 whiz kid, standing in front of a closed business that fooled him so completely. He wished he could disappear.

She was still eyeing him. "Yeah. I didn't recognize you without the trailer. You're the guy who bought Dappled Acres. Norm and I were having pie at the cafe in Sparrowsville last night and saw you cruise through town."

Oh. That was his new persona. No longer the corporate mogul. He was that dope who'd bought a piece of incinerated ground. He managed a nod. "Name's Rhett."

"Nice to meet you. I'm Betty." She adjusted the leash for her dog. "That took some guts, buying the place. A lightning strike burned the whole thing to cinders two years ago."

Guts? It was a colossal error, a move that required stupidity, a lack of diligence, and a supreme level of idiocy. It was the kind of decision he would have laughed at other people for making. She looked at him as if he should start explaining himself. What could he possibly say?

I was following God. At least, I thought I was.

While he struggled over the words, his phone rang. Saved by the bell. He excused himself and answered.

"Rhett, don't hang up on me." Don's voice was filled with a new conviction. "I've brokered the first phase of the deal and stalled them as long as I could. I need you here by Thursday. No excuses."

Rhett sighed.

"I know you're all giddy up there at the apple farm or whatever, but I've done some research, and it turns out there are plenty of places to grow things around here. Watsonville, Sebastopol, Marin County—and I have a Realtor on retainer who can make that happen in a heartbeat."

"I—"

"You can get your sister a piece of land and hire all the helping hands you need. Fly back and forth, for goodness' sake. You're a pilot, after all. She farms to her heart's content, and you get back to business where you belong."

Where you belong.

Uncertainty filled him, so strong he could taste it. He detested the feeling. It took him back to age fourteen when he'd watched helplessly as his mother drove away in their beat-up blue sedan and his father watched, motionless. Now a full-fledged grown-up, Rhett had been running around in trailers, arranging reunions that didn't work, buying ruined property, and making a mess of everything. All his plans ending in failure, defeat at every turn. He thought God had called him to do this. Called him to defeat and failure? Would God do that?

Maybe he'd been mistaken. Hugely, colossally, gigantically mistaken. He stared at his reflection in the glass on the front door. His hair was unruly, his shirt disheveled. Were those gaunt shadows under his cheekbones or a trick of the light? Who was the man staring back at him? Who was Rhett Hastings?

"I need to have a decision by Thursday," Don said. "Tell me you'll come back. Put me out of my misery. I can't take this anymore. I'm eating Tums by the fistful, and my wife says I'm as much fun as the crypt keeper."

"Don?"

"Yes?"

A beat of silence. "I'll call you by Thursday."

He glanced once more in the glass as he pocketed his phone. The woman and her dog had moved on, and he was alone with his reflection. He looked long and hard at the man staring back at him. *Who are you, Rhett Hastings?*

He was not sure how long he stood there, contemplating that stranger in the glass until he finally turned away.

Time to go back to his desolate apple orchard.

Time to admit to Karen and Stephanie what a fool he'd been about everything.

Twenty

Stephanie followed Karen as she wandered the orchard. After the chickens took themselves off to some secret location, Sweetness trailed along next to the women, sniffing and marking at will. Stephanie toted Panny, who was energized by new sights and smells, her button nose quivering.

"These were amazing trees. Red Delicious on the far end. They make good pollinating partners for the McIntosh apples, which were Grandad's pride and joy. Do you like McIntosh apples?"

"Um, I don't know. To be honest, I only pay attention to red and green or if it's in a pie or something. And strudel. One of the gals in my book club back in New York makes apple strudel. I don't know what apples she uses, but no one ever misses a meeting when it's strudel time. I've been known to bring my big purse just in case there's any left over."

Karen smiled. "You would know if you ate a McIntosh. Tart and sweet. Crisp white flesh." She stopped to finger a single green leaf sprouting from a blackened trunk. "Grandad would say his apples were just like life, sweet and sour at the same time. He was a bit of a poet. He loved old movies too. That's how Rhett got hooked on the cinema. They used to watch Bogart movies together until they had the lines memorized."

It made her happy to think of Rhett here at the farm, watching movies with his grandfather, living among these miraculous trees.

"I used to help with everything," Karen mused. "The picking and then making apple butter and pies. Granny always claimed she didn't really make a very good piecrust, so she'd ask her sister over, my Auntie Rhoda, and the two of them would talk and bake and laugh and drink coffee by the gallon." Karen smiled. "Oh, how they would laugh. I think Granny's piecrusts were just fine, but it was an excuse to see her sister, who would never think of dropping by without an invitation. It's funny how I can remember all those things when I can't recall people I met last week."

They followed the platoons of trees fanning out like shadow soldiers. Row after row of dead trunks appeared before them, a few bearing a hint of new growth here and there, spots of green amid the black. The grass underneath their feet had made a comeback, completely overtaking the sooty crust.

"Is it possible for the trees to recover?"

Karen took a penknife from her pocket and pried away a piece of the bark. Underneath, the wood was dry and parched. "This is the cambium layer where the growth happens." She shook her head and sighed. "Completely dried out and dead. Nothing can be done with these trees but to cut them down." Karen's mouth quivered as if she might cry.

"Is that what you're going to do?"

She cocked her head, staring into the dark forest. "I'm not sure yet. I don't make decisions as quickly as my brother, especially since I fell off that ladder and messed up my brain."

Stephanie figured she could use some of Karen's restraint. Her decisions were usually made in a snap and regretted for a much longer period of time. Ian used to save her from these off-the-cuff whims, like the time she'd agreed to run a day camp for four-year-olds and her brief desire to learn the trapeze.

Sweetness disappeared up the row of trees, following the swell of land as it dipped further down.

"Sweetness," Stephanie called. "Don't wander." She hastened forward to keep him in her line of vision. Cresting the highest point, she strained to see the dog but found something entirely different that froze her midstride.

"Karen, come here," she called.

Karen joined her, and they looked down onto a small pocket of trees, green and laden with baseball-sized apples. The overgrown canopy of branches intertwined above them, filtering the sunlight into a golden kaleidoscope. For a moment, all Stephanie could do was gaze in silence. The flames had decimated the trees all around, but somehow, this little oasis of fifty or so trees had survived.

Karen plucked off one of the fruits. "They're McIntoshes! Can you believe it?" She laughed, sniffing the fruit. "My word. Dappled Acres still has some life in her after all." Karen tossed the apple high into the blue sky. Sweetness barked with glee and chased after it, making a neat catch and gobbling down the fruit.

Stephanie put Panny on the grass, and the little dog tottered along for a few steps before she sat, nose deep in the turf. Sweetness joined her, and together they enjoyed the symphony of invisible fragrances, rubbing their chins on the carpet of grass.

Stephanie breathed in the scent of the trees. The morning temperature was giving way to a warm summer day. Sitting here in the mini orchard that had escaped the blitzkrieg, she could imagine what it must have been like when Dappled Acres was a thriving farm where Karen and Rhett found freedom from their mother's abandonment and their father's harsh rules.

But what about now? Would Rhett force Mr. Phipps to reverse the sale? And then what? Find another farm for Karen? Something in the bleak look on his face when he'd left made her doubt. How could he reconcile this setback with the plan he'd thought had been laid out by God? What happened when you marched forward, armed with the knowledge that God was on your side, only to fall squarely on your face?

Sweetness came over and offered his back for some scratching. She complied. *How easy it is to make a dog happy,* she thought. *Is it because they don't insist on making plans? They take life as it comes—the good, the bad, and everything in between.* Her own plans had gotten muddled, for sure, but her goal was still intact, her dream just a few hundred miles away. Rhett's was not even in one piece anymore.

"Stephanie," Karen said suddenly. "Do you know how to hook up a trailer?"

"Not a clue. Why?"

"Rhett said there's water and electricity to the house. I think I saw some extension cords in the trailer. I remember Uncle Mel used to connect the trailer up to the farmhouse sometimes when he would come for a long visit."

"I'll search it on YouTube," Stephanie said. "But does this mean you and Rhett are going to stay here? In spite of the...er...damage?"

Karen smiled. "I can't speak for Rhett, but I'm going to stay, at least for a while, and Panny and I will require air-conditioning. Are you in?"

Stephanie scooped up Panny and fell in step behind Karen. Determination must be a family trait, she decided. "I'm in," she said. *At least until it's time for me to go.*

∾

He'd practiced what to say on the long ride back to Dappled Acres. Best to say it straight out. Karen would understand. How could she not see the truth written on every blackened twig and branch? His speech went out the window as he parked next to the trailer, which appeared to be hooked up via some extension cords to the old farmhouse.

Stephanie and Karen sat outside on lawn chairs, sketching something out on a piece of paper. With a sinking feeling, he joined them.

"What are you doing? Why did you two hook up the trailer?"

Stephanie arched an eyebrow. "You're supposed to say, 'Wow, that's amazing how you made this all happen in my absence. Gee whiz, aren't you both terribly clever?'"

He was not about to be charmed out of making the right decision. "We're not staying here. We'll pack up, and I'll drop you and Sweetness at Agnes Wharton's house just like I promised. Then Karen and I will head back to California."

Karen's lips thinned. "I see you've worked it all out. Does Karen get a vote in this, or is she to be carted around like the dogs?"

Rhett squared his shoulders. "This place is ruined."

"Some of the trees survived," she said. "There's a section of fifty McIntosh trees in perfect condition."

"Doesn't matter. The rest of the orchard will have to be replanted, the house rebuilt. It will take years for it to become profitable, if ever."

Karen waved a hand as if she were brushing away a fly. "What else have I got to do?"

He gaped at her. "You can't do this. You're not strong enough."

"I am aware of that, brother. I will hire people, and no, you will not have to pay. I have some money stashed away, and there are such things as loans."

"It's not about the money—"

"I know, but I've never taken charity from you before, and I'm not going to start now. Though it will take time, I will buy the property from you." She sat back, smiling.

Stephanie's eyes were round. She looked as though she would like to be anywhere else. Rhett felt the same.

"The orchard," he repeated slowly, "is ruined."

Karen flapped a piece of paper at him. "But the land isn't. We can revive it. Stephanie and I have been making a priority list. First off, we'll need to do what we can for the McIntoshes. It's too late for pruning, of course, but we can tidy them up. We'll take out the dead trees a little at a time, and I'll see if anything can be salvaged of the farmhouse. We have two chickens if I can catch them. There's nothing better than eggs from free range chickens, don't you think?"

Two sets of maddeningly determined female eyes regarded him. "This isn't rational."

"Nothing you've done recently has been rational, Rhett. You let God lead the way, remember?"

"But He *isn't* leading the way," Rhett spat, his anger boiling over. "Everything has turned to ashes sifting through my fingers. It was a mistake to leave my business, it was lunacy to think that Paulo..." He stopped and took a breath. "And it was a blunder to buy this place, the worst business decision I've ever made. The whole trailer trip has been one tremendous mess-up from start to finish."

Karen folded her hands on her lap. "So was it a blunder for me to let you back in my life then? To forgive you for what you did to me and Paulo?"

He rubbed a hand across his face.

Her mouth quivered. "You and I, we're siblings again. Was all of that just the by-product of a deal gone bad?"

Stephanie got up. "I'm just going to go into the trailer and fix a snack."

"No," Karen said. "You've been in this from the beginning. Tell Rhett that he's got to let go and trust God, just like he's been trying to do."

Rhett shook his head. "Don't drag her into this."

"Why not? She's part of this journey you've been on."

"She's just here for the ride."

Stephanie flinched. He'd hurt her. Well, why not? It was true that she was along purely for the transportation. Klein and the mythical Gregory needed a new agent, which was the only reason she was still on the ridiculous adventure. Agent Stephanie Pink would probably not ever breathe a word of the strange path she'd had to take to get her name on the office door. Or maybe she'd have a few good laughs remembering the lunatic guy she'd happened upon on her way to landing the deal that made her career.

A part of him deep down inside longed to be contradicted. In his fevered imagination he could almost hear her say it. *You're not crazy, Rhett. And you're not just a man on a fruitless mission, a means to an end. You're much more than that to me.*

Her eyes searched his and, coward that he was, he looked away.

"This doesn't involve me," she said quietly. "I'll go get that snack now."

He watched her go, and his heart plummeted to his shoes.

Karen was staring at him when he ventured at look at her.

"Rhett, for a corporate genius, you are a real numbskull."

He agreed inside, but he forced a strong tone. "You can't stay here on this farm alone."

"I'll hire help," her tone softened. "But I thought we were going to bring Dappled Acres back to life together."

"There's no life here to revive, sis," he said softly. "This was a mistake, nothing more. You're blinded by sentiment."

"And you're blinded by business." She laughed. "So let's be two blind numbskulls together and trust God to make it work out."

"I can't. I misheard God. This has been a monumental failure."

"Oh, I think people can learn a lot about God through their failures."

The conversation was going nowhere. He shoved a hand through his hair. "I got you back in spite of my idiocies, and for that I'll always be grateful, but this has been a losing proposition from the get-go. I was thinking it was part of that 'plans to give you hope and a future' thing from Jeremiah. I was wrong."

"Rhett Franklin Hastings," Karen said, eyes blazing. "You wouldn't know what prosperity was if it marched up and bit you on the nose."

"What are you talking about?"

"I'm talking about this," she waved an arm around. "The orchard, the trees that lived, Stephanie, all of it."

"I don't understand what you're getting at."

"No, you sure don't, Rhett." Throwing her notes on the ground, she snatched up her cane and stalked back into the trailer, slamming the door behind her.

Panny looked up from her blanket, and Sweetness sent a reproachful glance toward him.

"What do *you* know?" he snapped. "All you have in the world is a spatula."

Twenty-One

Stephanie had gone out to the orchard to sit among the living trees with Sweetness while Panny enjoyed an afternoon nap with Karen. After checking for snakes, she sat on a fallen trunk and considered. She'd tried to place a call to Mr. Klein while back at the trailer, but in this otherworldly spot her phone wouldn't acquire a signal. Fitting, it seemed to her. This little pocket of life seemed so far removed from everything practical. She had three books with her, *Sea Comes Knocking, From the Mixed-Up Files of Mrs. Basil E. Frankweiler*, and an odd little story about a woman who solved mysteries while tending a flock of seagulls, bought for a quarter at their last supply stop.

The sound of rustling leaves played the perfect counterpoint for reading. In her bookstore, she decided, there would be an area for kids to read with trees painted on the walls and a forest of bookshelves. And maybe big green pillows sewn to look like leaves where kids could get lost in a story as she and Ian had done so many times. She breathed in the sweet scent of growing fruit and the smell of musty pages as she opened *Sea Comes Knocking*.

I look with bewilderment at this rugged place where I am somehow rooted. I am not a country girl, I cry to the mountains. I was not made to grieve a dead child, I wail to the cloud-glazed sky. I do not want to love a man who cannot be free while wearing the fetters of civilization. I did not choose these things, I chant to the wind. I did not choose.

They were chosen for you, a flock of geese replies as they escape the coming winter.

Stephanie was only six pages away from the end of the book, and she didn't have to continue. She knew the memoir ended with Agnes pregnant and Jedd gone, having left to work his fishing boat. The scene took place on the heels of an intense argument between the two. Agnes had not revealed her pregnancy to Jedd. He had not looked back as he'd left her. Had their marriage survived? Had the baby? It was the greatest mystery of the decade, and one she was about to solve as soon as she took possession of the second manuscript.

Sweetness noticed Rhett's approach first, bounding to greet him and threatening to jump up and mark Rhett's midriff with dusty paw prints. Rhett fended him off and sat down on a log opposite Stephanie.

"Okay if I join you?"

"It's your orchard."

He sighed. "That it is. Every blighted acre of it." He plucked a strand of grass and twisted it between his fingers. He looked fatigued. Worry lines grooved into his forehead, and a five o'clock shadow darkened his chin. "I've called Bethany. She's coming up tonight to stay with Karen for a few days so I'll be able to drive you to Agnes Wharton's place tomorrow. Is that too late?"

"You don't have to do that. I'll get a ride."

"A deal's a deal."

She wondered why that phrase hurt. "Not everything in life is a deal, Rhett. You helped me. I will always appreciate that."

He looked as though he wanted to say something, but he

remained silent, staring off into the blackened trees behind them. "I see all this ruin, but I still can't believe it."

Sweetness alerted on some sound they couldn't hear and trotted into the long grass, leaving the circle of life for the dead zone.

She stood. "Come here for a minute," she said, walking to him. He stood. "What?"

"You're looking at the wrong thing." Taking his arm she turned him in the direction of the McIntosh trees. "See? If you look this way, you can see what was spared, the life that's still here." She didn't know why, but she felt a deep urgency to make him understand. "It's what your sister sees."

He stared at the green oasis, the rays of sunlight playing across his face. "It's not enough."

"Maybe you're counting it wrong. This journey you've been on was enough to bring you and your sister together. This place is enough to give her purpose and passion. Maybe it could be enough for you too."

His gaze fastened on hers. "Life isn't like your novels, Stephanie. Reality is much uglier."

"That's why people love novels. Fiction tosses up the truth about life that we're too blind or preoccupied to see."

He rubbed his eyes. "It wasn't supposed to be like this."

"Story of my life. Nothing ever is."

He reached out a hand and smoothed her hair, trailing his fingers along her cheek. Her body responded to his touch, and she put her hand over his, cradling his palm to her cheek.

"Why do you mix me up inside?" he murmured.

"Part of my charm, I guess."

"You know, Spencer was an idiot to let you go."

It was the kindest thing anyone had ever said to her.

He put his mouth to her forehead, and she stayed breathlessly still as he traced his lips along her cheek and temple. She tipped her chin, and he kissed her, a tender, sweet connection that made her heart swell.

What was he doing? Why was she enjoying it? She wanted to pull away but found that she couldn't.

He leaned his cheek against hers and let out a deep breath before straightening. "Someday you'll find someone who will love you properly."

And just like that, the wild feelings inside her stilled.

He kept hold of her hand, though, and together they watched a sparrow land on a branch, snatching up an insect from the roughened bark before taking flight again.

"Karen thinks Dappled Acres can be saved," Stephanie said, still feeling the tingles from his touch, the sadness that it was fleeting.

"She's wrong."

"What if she's not? We talked it over, Rhett. She has some really good ideas. They are practical and not merely pie-in-the-sky."

He released her hand and took a step back. "Please don't encourage Karen in this."

"Why not? I care about her."

"I do too. That's why I'm going to get her to leave this place."

"But it's her dream—"

"Don't talk to me about dreams!"

"Dreams are all your sister has."

"Then she needs to wise up. Dreaming is impractical and confusing, and pretty soon you can't tell which ones are the ones God wants you to have or the ones you come up with on your own."

"You're upset because you didn't know about the condition of the orchard."

"No, I'm upset because you're a hypocrite."

She jerked, a hot spot igniting inside. "That's meaner than usual. How so?"

"You still insist that your dream is to be a literary agent and run a high-powered business in New York City. You think that's what God wants for you?"

"That's what I want for me."

"Your skill set doesn't match your desire."

"What's that supposed to mean?"

"You're about as far removed from a high-powered businessperson as anyone could be."

"I am not!"

"You put smiley emoticons on all your texts and e-mails."

"That's called being friendly, not your area of expertise."

"You organize your life with sticky notes, and you are not clear on the bottom line."

"I'm an out-of-the-box thinker."

"You eat bologna and cheese."

"So I'm not a food snob. Who cares?"

"You don't read the highbrow books you're supposed to like. Instead, you read romance novels and fiction with sea monsters on the covers."

She folded her arms and glared at him. "At least I *read*."

"And you love books more than business, and you love your brother so much you've convinced yourself his plan has to be yours."

She struggled for breath. "You don't know anything about it."

He would not let her look away. "And you're too stubborn or too scared to admit that you're living your whole life to make your brother's plan come to fruition."

She was shaking now. "Stop it, Rhett! Don't try to ruin my plan just because yours didn't work out."

"And you're leaving. After tomorrow, we're not a part of your life anymore, right? You're off to become Agent Pink."

"That's right," she said, voice breaking. "That was the whole point of riding with you, remember? Just along for the ride."

"Yeah. I remember," he said, voice suddenly weary and soft. "So do me a favor, and don't give my sister any of your advice."

She met his gaze and saw her own troubled expression mirrored in his eyes. "I'm sorry your plans didn't work out, Rhett. I really am."

She felt him staring at her as she left. Mercifully, the tears did not come until after she'd left him behind in the unexpected pocket of green.

He was up before the sun with Sweetness by his side. Later on he and Stephanie and Sweetness would start the long drive to Agnes Wharton's, and part of him didn't want to head out on the last leg of their journey. He'd been cruel, though he didn't understand why. What did it matter to him if she ran after the agent's job? Her life, not his. *Just along for the ride.* Still, he didn't want their last shared miles to be thick with anger and hurt. He would figure out what to say to make it right. She'd taught him a few things about being kind.

God, if there's any part of this mess that can be salvaged, give me the words. But why would He? Rhett had spent hours staring at the wall of the trailer, and he'd come to the conclusion that he was a hijacker. Instead of letting God lead the way, he'd taken the divine urge he'd felt and used it as an excuse to fashion a set of marching orders and enact his own set of meticulous plans.

Not one of which had remotely worked out.

Humbled. It was a sensation Rhett Hastings did not enjoy and never had. It left him with a slightly sick feeling, and a sense of anxiety which he was not sure how to salve. His fingers closed around the phone in his pocket. One call to Don, and he could fit his life back together again.

Sweetness dashed out of the tall grass where he'd been nosing and barked at Rhett.

"I don't speak dog. Haven't we covered that?"

Sweetness barked again, pranced away a few steps, and then came back.

"All right," Rhett said. "But if this is another rescue, I'm not in the mood." Nonetheless, he followed Sweetness, swishing through the shin-high carpet until he came upon an oval nest of grasses lined with downy gray fur. Rabbits, most likely, though the nest was unoccupied.

"That's very interesting, Sweetness. Thanks for sharing."

The dog gave him what could only be described as a look reserved for idiots and barked at a spot a few feet away. Rhett dutifully followed and found a baby rabbit, its eyes closed, its tiny ears tucked back against its body. The creature was not even as big as his palm.

"I guess someone got left behind," he said, leaning close to confirm that the fragile ribs were rising and falling. "It's best to leave it here, Sweetness. It will get eaten by a snake or something and be part of the food chain."

Sweetness licked the bunny from tiny tail to quivering nose.

"It's not going to live anyway, probably. Circle of life stuff."

Now a bark.

"Look, dog. We can't be rescuing half dead creatures everywhere we go. It's just not practical. This thing is weak, and it's not going to survive. It was a miracle that Panny did. Face the facts, why don't you? Some things you can't change."

Another bark and a madly wiggling rump.

"Oh, knock it off."

The dog fired off several more barks.

"I'm not a nice man, Sweetness. Haven't you got that yet? I'm the kind who swallows up businesses and orders people around and takes my own way instead of God's way." *And calls women hypocrites. One-of-a-kind women who do not deserve such treatment.*

Sweetness cocked his head, his brown eyes guileless. What did a dog know of human failure? He just kept looking at you without bringing up your past or expecting you to do the right thing. The optimism for those who so richly did not deserve it astounded him. What did a dog know?

"I'm not the man you think I am," he said, turning and walking away. He looked behind him one more time. Sweetness sat heavily on the grass.

"I've got to fuel the truck and make a phone call."

And then he walked away.

Twenty-Two

Stephanie waited under the shade of a sprawling buckeye for Jack Wershing to show up. He did at precisely one thirty. She calculated the timing as she climbed onto the front seat, Sweetness sandwiched next to her. According to Google, they would arrive at Agnes Wharton's just before eight p.m. She would not expect Jack to wait for her to conclude her business. Somehow, she would arrange a way to an airport with her precious manuscript in hand. That should be easy because she would no longer have Sweetness. She forced her clenched stomach muscles to relax.

The dog was anxious, whining and trying to get a good look at Karen and Panny. Karen and Stephanie had decided together that the old dog should stay on at the orchard. Panny still needed too much care. They couldn't ask Agnes to provide that. She cranked the window down.

Karen handed over Sweetness's spatula, which he accepted with a whimper of pleasure. Jack raised an eyebrow but stoically kept his gaze directed out the front window.

"Thank you for everything, Karen." Stephanie clasped the woman's hand. "I know you're going to make a success of Dappled Acres."

"Yes, I will. And I'll take good care of Panny. You are invited to come back and visit anytime you have a break in your agent duties."

Stephanie scanned the orchard. There was still no sign of Rhett.

"He's gone to town. He said to tell you he'd be back in an hour to take you."

"It's better this way."

Karen's mouth twitched. "Is it?"

She stared until Stephanie felt herself flushing. "Rhett and I have different plans."

"He doesn't know what his real plans are and he's scared, so he's defaulting to what's comfortable. Business, winning, profit—things like that."

Stephanie understood. *Rhett, I hope you find what you're looking for.*

"I've been thinking a lot about Rhett since we left Bethany's house. I was so angry with him for such a long time."

"You had your reasons."

"I did. How ironic that I couldn't remember what they were until he reminded me." She stroked Panny. "He didn't have to tell me, and before, he probably wouldn't have, but he's changed. God's giving him new marching orders, and he's struggling with that."

"He needs time."

"I agree. Stay here for a while. You're good for him. You can help him figure it out."

"I'm not the person to do that, Karen. God and I are barely on speaking terms."

"Come on, Stephanie. He's a guy who googles grace and is scared to set foot in a church because he might have to sing in public and eat Jell-O salad at potlucks. This is a man who needs all the help he can get."

Stephanie giggled, but Karen did not join in. Her eyes were troubled, so like her brother's.

"I think I've gotten some sort of perspective on life, after the U-turn and losing Paulo. I've decided I'm going to say what's on my mind and heart, even if it's unpopular."

Stephanie grimaced. "Should I brace myself?"

She shrugged. "All I'm going to say is that you two are so busy writing your own stories, you can't see that God put you together for a reason."

Stephanie blinked and shook her head. She wanted to roll up the window against that stream of honesty. What reason could there be for her zany adventure with Rhett? What plan? God wasn't in that. And if He was, she certainly hadn't asked Him to be, so He could jolly well butt out again. "I have a job to finish."

Karen cocked her head. "What would happen if you didn't finish it?"

For a second she thought about what it would be like to let go of her name on the door of Klein and Gregory, to back away from that desire that had turned into her sole focus. Would it be freeing? Would she feel a new joy fill her spirit? But that was the way of letting go of many things—Ian's dream, her distrust of God. Something deep inside her quivered with longing and with fear. She wobbled for an instant between two worlds, poised on a knife blade of uncertainty.

The seconds stretched between them. Then, "I have to go, Karen. I'm sorry. I really am."

Karen nodded sadly. "Okay. I wish you well, Stephanie. I'm going to pray for you."

She thought suddenly of Mrs. Granato at the beginning of the zany adventure, the sweet lady who was no doubt praying for Stephanie as well. Mrs. Granato, Karen, the ladies at the Chain Gang. All part of her story, all praying not for the swift completion of her job, but that she, Stephanie Pink, might live the life that God meant for her.

She gripped the door handle. This was the final moment when Stephanie Pink could change her destiny and cancel the plans made so long ago. She thought about Rhett and the curls of his hair, the sincere way he was trying to learn to be nice, the incredible courage it must have taken to walk away from his business and trust the God he did not fully know, one she didn't either.

Sweetness stuck his head out the window and licked Panny, who nuzzled him back. She remembered the triumph on Rhett's face when the ruined dog had stood for the first time, and her heart ached.

Fear, excitement, and love whirled together. "I'm sorry, Karen," she murmured again. "Take good care of Panny."

Karen smiled. Sweetness whined again, his paws pressed into her lap as he tried to exit the truck, knocking loose the slobbery spatula. "It's okay, Sweetness. You'll come back here someday."

It was a lie even she did not believe. She handed Sweetness his chewed spatula, and he took it solemnly in his mouth as she rolled up the window, shutting out the smells of the orchard, the soft coo of the chickens, and the cool wind of change.

"Ready?" Jack said.

"Ready," she answered.

∽

Rhett returned with a full tank of gas and an odd assortment of items, including goat's milk, a medicine dropper, and some soft towels. On the way back he stopped in the dilapidated barn and cleaned out an old wooden crate he'd seen there, lining it with the soft towel before he went in search of the rabbit. He was surprised that Sweetness had not come out to help him and felt foolish that he wanted him to.

"You're going soft in the head, Hastings." Why had he changed his mind about saving the rabbit anyway? He didn't know, but his heart seemed to beat a softer rhythm recently, his soul echoing with sweeter notes. Maybe it was the nostalgia of returning to Dappled Acres or the joy at having his sister in his life again. Or maybe it was born from spending time with Stephanie Pink, a woman who made him want to be better. With a start, he realized it was the thought of her and not bunnies that had made him return.

Stephanie's words came back to him, a tender memory shared over bites of rubbery bologna. *I realized I was alone and my brother wasn't coming back. I felt as if I would always be alone from then on, as if I'd been the one bird left in the nest after all the rest had flown away for the winter.*

The one bird left in the nest. He'd imagined it might be the same for this bunny. Opening its little black eyes to find it was the one left behind, too weak to follow, too scared to move.

Did Stephanie still feel like that? Left behind and too scared to find her own way?

"God?" he prayed, but couldn't get any further. God...but how should he pray when he was not sure of his own way? His life was turning out to be so completely different than he'd ever dreamed. Shaking away the troubling thoughts, he retraced the path Sweetness had shown him.

It took a bit of searching until he found the bunny, still motionless and burrowed into the grass where he'd left it. Sinking down onto his knees, he cupped the tiny thing in his hands, marveling at the silkiness of the fur as he tucked the baby in the soft blanket liner and headed to the trailer. He wondered what crazy name Stephanie would come up with for the newest oddball member of the tribe.

She's leaving.

He'd been repeating it to himself all morning.

She's leaving.

Yet the reminders did not help him untangle her from his

thoughts. Determined, he tucked the box under his arm, keeping an eye out for Sweetness and Stephanie. Back at the trailer, he opened the door to find Karen sitting with Panny and sipping a cup of coffee. He lifted up the blanket-wrapped rabbit and introduced it to Panny, who perked up instantly, her tail whipping.

"Are we nursing another patient?" Karen asked.

"Looks that way."

Karen took the bunny and settled it next to Panny. Panny prodded and poked the animal, rolling it closer to herself until she snuggled it against her belly like a mother hen warming an egg.

"Do you think Panny realizes it's not a dog?" Rhett said.

Karen shrugged. "She's going to need something to replace Sweetness. She's been moping since they left."

Rhett jerked. "Left?"

"They're gone," Karen said. "Stephanie took Sweetness while you were in town. She called Jack to give her a ride to Agnes Wharton's. She left you a note."

He picked up a folded piece of paper from the table. Next to the note was a neat pile of bills and coins along with an itemized list written on a napkin.

Here's what I owe you. I put in three extra dollars for the bologna because I know you aren't going to eat it. Thank you for everything. Steph

The payment amounted to thirty-two dollars and seventeen cents. He stared at the stack of money and the messily scrawled note.

Thank you for everything.

What had he given her other than a delay that might cost her the manuscript? A hard time about her goal to be a literary agent? An attitude regarding bologna and white bread? Unkind remarks from an insensitive clod?

He was struck by a sudden thought. What if God meant for their two lives to be woven together?

Twin flames of wonder and disbelief burned through him as he realized he was opening his eyes, like a baby rabbit who had discovered he was alone in the nest, the others having hopped away.

Too weak to follow.

Too scared to move.

Stephanie Pink was meant to be in his life, nestled in his heart. God put her there, but Rhett had been too focused on his plans to notice.

Too late! his heart screamed. *It's too late.*

In a blink of an eye, he was left with the comfort of thirty-two dollars and seventeen cents.

Just like that, Stephanie Pink and Sweetness were out of his life for good.

Twenty-Three

Stephanie stayed awake for most of the journey. The road unwound in looping spirals far into the mountains. She marveled at the rugged beauty of it for the first couple of hours. Then the sameness of it all, the miles of serenity, made her long for the honk of a taxi or the endless parade of feet on rain-soaked sidewalks. *It will be good to get back to New York,* she told herself.

She would tell her roommate, Sass, and the Chain Gang all about the madcap adventure, about Sweetness and Panny, and about the feral cat.

About Rhett. Her heart thudded painfully. Maybe not about him, not at first, until she had time to decide how many pages he would fill in her life story, the number of incredible scenes she would never in a trillion years forget.

Jack was not a talker. He was perfectly content to listen to soft country music on the radio, drumming his calloused fingers on the steering wheel.

She'd thanked him profusely several times, and each time he'd shrugged as if he was merely giving her a lift across town, so they'd settled upon a silence that made her tense.

What if she was making the arduous journey only to discover she was too late? That Laura had already scooped her and stolen the manuscript? Sweetness stirred next to her and she knew she would make the trip anyway. Though she'd grown to love the dog, if she were honest with herself, she knew Sweetness belonged heart and soul to someone else who missed him dearly.

Thanks, God, for loaning him to me. Her prayer surprised her. The enormous, ungainly animal had dragged her along through puddles of joy, patches of laughter, and moments of tenderness, and she was better for having known him. And Panny. And Karen and Rhett.

She squeezed her hands together to stop her mind from careening away again. *Would you, for one pea-picking moment, focus on the job you've come three thousand miles to do?*

God, she silently prayed. *Stephanie Pink here. Uh, I know we haven't spoken at length in a while—a very long while. But I need that novel, so, um, if You feel like it, I would appreciate Your helping me get this dog to Agnes Wharton. I am so close to having our plans turn out, mine and Ian's. Rhett says I'm only doing this for Ian, but he doesn't understand...*

For one thunderstruck moment, she felt confused, as if she did not understand either, this dream she had clung to for so long.

She heard Rhett's voice, saying the words softly, the words in which he'd put his trust. *"I know the plans I have for you,"* declares the LORD, *"plans to prosper you and not to harm you, plans to give you hope and a future."*

But her plan was better. Unless it wasn't. God wanted the best for her? If she could only believe it. Her future, her hope, her name written upon some imaginary door, her own door, her own threshold. But she could still hear the echoes of that door slamming shut the day her brother died, closing against a God who allowed an unbearable hurt, an incurable wound.

Yet lately, had she not felt the stirrings of connection again? Spurred by Rhett? A man she probably could love if circumstances were completely different. Love him? Prickles erupted on her skin.

Still suspended in the middle of her prayer, she wanted to say more, but her thoughts trailed off into confusion. Best to stop. In novels as in prayers, it didn't pay to clutter up the narrative. *I guess that's it for now, God,* she said silently. *Pink signing off.*

As she got to the *Amen,* Sweetness sat up, sensing that Jack was slowing. There, on the narrow shoulder of the road, stood a woman with limp hair sticking out under a cloche hat. Stephanie went cold. Literary agent Laura Burns. She stood with one finger to her ear, a phone pressed against the other. Jack pulled to a stop.

"What are you doing?" Stephanie demanded.

He looked at her in surprise. "She needs help. No services around here for miles."

Before Stephanie could say another word, Jack was out of the car.

Laura beamed a dazzling smile at him. "Thanks for stopping. I'm out of gas. This rental car sucks up fuel like a camel drinks water."

Stephanie hopped out of the truck as well, and all her frustration flooded right past her internal filter. "Serves you right, trying to poach my manuscript."

Laura's eyes widened and then narrowed. "Pink. I thought I might have made a wrong turn, but I see now I'm headed right to victory."

"Oh no, you're not. Agnes Wharton is my client."

Laura laughed. "This isn't the good old days, honey. All's fair in love and literature. Winner gets the spoils and all that."

"We have a verbal agreement with Agnes Wharton."

"So? She'll sign with whomever gives her a better deal and you know it."

Jack stared from woman to woman, and he then headed to the back of his truck for the gas can secured there.

"Stop! You can't give her the gas, Jack," Stephanie said, her hands on her hips. "She's a poacher."

Laura pointed at Stephanie. "Don't get in the way of a Good Samaritan. I'm pretty sure that's in the Ten Commandments."

Jack stood frozen as he mulled it over. "Ain't right to leave her stranded," he decided, moving to Laura's car.

Stephanie's ears buzzed and her pulse pounded in her temples. Not now, not when she was so close. Her self-control snapped like a dry dog biscuit, and she ran to Jack's truck, grabbed her purse, and tossed it to him. He caught it one handed, his mouth open in surprise.

"That's my purse, wallet, and cell phone. I'm sorry, Jack. I promise I'll bring it back."

He blinked. "Bring what back?"

"Your truck," she said, hopping into the driver's seat, gunning the engine, and barreling up the road toward 1 Eagle Cliff Road.

∞

Rhett chopped away at the burned branches. The ax felt good in his hands. It released some stress and helped him focus on the looming problem. Karen. She stood stubbornly by the position that she would work the farm, regardless of the impossibility of the task, the ridiculous amount of work it would require, the physical toll it would take. She was already making appointments with bankers to discuss a loan.

"Before I left Hastings Cinemas, I arranged for a trust fund for you," he tried to tell her. "You're taken care of. You don't need a loan."

She waved him away. "I'll save it for my old age. You're not going to support me financially."

He both lamented and admired her determination. It was the

same stubborn attitude that allowed him to build a business empire from nothing. As he whacked away at the charred tree that was leaning precariously toward the old farmhouse, he heard Bethany and Karen sitting outside the trailer, cooing over the baby rabbit. They'd christened it Bunny. Bunny and Panny. His life was turning into a nursery rhyme. They'd dutifully fed the infant rabbit some goat's milk from the dropper under the watchful eye of Panny, who was pleased to lick the baby clean between each mouthful.

Karen was right. Panny really did seem to need a fuzzy companion since Sweetness was gone. He heard Bethany laugh, and he was grateful she'd decided she might as well stay for a few days since she'd driven all the way over.

It would give him some freedom to get workmen in to trim the trees, and a contractor to quote a price to rehab the farmhouse. Karen would complain that he was butting in. And he was. And he would, until Thursday when he'd return to San Francisco and leave Dappled Acres far behind.

Would he really be able to drive away and leave his sister here on a broken-down farm fifty miles from the nearest doctor? What was the other option? Stay and help her? He knew nothing about trees or harvests or tilling the soil. It was preposterous.

He put down the ax and wandered away into the black trees standing sentry on their carpet of green. The sun was warm, and sweat dampened his forehead. It would have made a grand movie, this whole ridiculous RV journey from Big Thumb to Dappled Acres, collecting animals along the way. And what would the final scene be? The hero returning to the life he knew, changed certainly. A better man, hopefully. *That is not such a bad ending after all,* he told himself. He'd come often to help his sister and check in on her constantly. He could talk to experts who might be able to advise them on things farming related. The plan comforted him, yet there was still a hollow, empty feeling in his heart that he could not shake. Maybe he never would.

His gaze drifted to the distant tangle of green, and he walked there, drawn by the scent of fruit. The breeze ruffled the leaves and set them dancing, cooling his skin at the same time. The two chickens paraded by, unconcerned now that Sweetness was not around to stalk them, scrabbling and pecking at the earth.

Sweetness probably would have shimmied up to the nearest tree, scratched himself against the bark, and then thrown himself down in a patch of sunlight to relish the warmth streaming through the canopy.

He kept his face toward the green, remembering Stephanie's words. *"See? If you look this way you can see what was spared, the life that's still here...it's what your sister sees."*

But the cost of restoring all these trees? The years it would take to resurrect this old orchard? What Karen saw was beyond even the scope of rose-colored glasses.

The sun broke through the waving branches, etching a pathway of light and painting the orchard in golden splendor. And then, in an instant, the light got inside Rhett Hastings, gilding him with a splendid revelation. *It's not about the trees*, he thought suddenly. The plan he'd heard so clearly, God's plan, was strong and undeniable, but he'd got one tiny word wrong, the name.

"Change Karen's life," he'd heard.

He realized his mistake in that sunlit moment, in the apple-scented threshold between the dead trees and the living. God had not just given him the opportunity to restore Karen's life, but his own.

He understood at last what God was trying to tell him.

Come close to Me, and I will reinvent your life in ways you've never imagined, better than any plan you could dream up.

He'd started by depositing Rhett squarely in the middle of a decimated property, side by side with his sister, a farm that needed him, filled with broken buildings and oddball critters.

The blue of the sky dazzled his eyes as he looked up at a patchwork of azure, emerald green leaves, and the barest puff of downy white clouds. The strange fact was, it didn't matter if the orchard ever became profitable or not. It did not matter that all his strategies and plotting had come to nothing. He was a different man, a better man. Suddenly, abruptly, fantastically, unbelievably, Rhett Hastings understood.

He laughed, offering up the sound to the branches, wishing Sweetness were there to join him in a merry game of chase. *Finally*, the dog would say. *You are a very dim-witted human.*

Rhett was seized by a desire as strong as the fire that had swept through his grandfather's apple trees. He had to tell Stephanie Pink what he had learned.

It was ridiculous, really, his brain said. She was probably on her way to New York, manuscript in hand, Sweetness safely delivered.

She would think him crazy, perhaps. Maybe he was, but he knew he had to tell her, had to show her that she'd been right all along. Maybe it would change her life in some small way too.

"I've gotta go," he shouted to Karen and Bethany as he cleared the orchard.

Both women looked up, startled.

"Where?" Karen asked.

"To find Stephanie!" he hollered. "I'll explain later."

Something in the knowing glance they gave each other made him think they already knew more about his unaccountable actions than he did. Paying no mind, he raced to the truck. He'd just gotten his fingers around the door's handle when a vehicle pulled in behind him.

A police car.

Out stepped a cop.

He was not smiling.

"Mr. Hastings," he said, "I need to have a word."

Twenty-Four

Stephanie wondered how long the jail sentence might possibly be for driving with a suspended license. Or stealing a truck.

"It wasn't actually stealing," she told Sweetness. He looked encouragingly at her. "I left my purse as collateral. That makes it sort of a barter, right?"

He offered a consoling lick to her forearm.

"You're a good dog, Sweetness. You know that?"

He took that as encouragement to sidle over and extend his tongue further, bathing her upper arm as well.

"All right," she said with a laugh and a gentle shove. "You'll be home to lick Agnes in no time."

The remaining ten miles were steep. Her apprehension grew with each jostling turn. Agnes would no doubt be overjoyed at having Sweetness back, but would she be irate at the delay? Would she take the dog, slam the door, and send Stephanie packing?

She imagined what Mr. Klein would say.

"Ms. Pink, get that manuscript. No excuses."

Clenching the steering wheel, she started up a gravel driveway, past a surprisingly modern mailbox, and on up the steep slope. Trees crowded around so thick it might have been dusk. A couple of quail regarded her curiously from their spots under the bushes, earning an interested glance from Sweetness.

The driveway crested the slope and dropped down into a hollow. Set back behind a well-tended rock garden, was 1 Eagle Cliff Road.

Stephanie did a double take. The neatly painted, tile-roofed house with the two-car garage was not what she had been expecting. It should be something rustic, a homestead hewn by Jedd and Agnes with their own hands, made of logs with a moss-covered roof.

This structure had painted aluminum gutters and a badminton net erected in the side lawn. Could she have made a mistake? Eccentric authors who lived off the grid didn't have such modern-looking domiciles. But there on the house was a shiny brass number 1, and she'd seen the sign for Eagle Cliff Road.

No more stalling. She parked the truck and got out, clipped Sweetness to the leash, and marched up to the doorway, her heart pounding. She rang the bell and heard melodious chimes sounding inside.

Butterflies somersaulted through her chest as someone approached the door.

"This is it, Sweetness. We're finally here."

Sweetness wriggled his hindquarters, and she noticed he still had the spatula in his mouth. Now she could finally ask Agnes about that weird fetish.

The door swung open.

"Hello," she said brightly. "I..."

A small man with his hand on the knob was wearing khakis and a tucked-in polo shirt. His mostly bald head had a fringe of hair circling the wider portions. Reading glasses slid low on his nose, magnifying his brown eyes.

"Hello," he said, eyeing her and the dog. "Can I help you? Did you have some car trouble?"

"Uh, no. No car trouble. I'm bringing him home." She pointed to Sweetness.

The man peered over the top of his glasses. "Why does he have a spatula in his mouth?"

"I was hoping to ask you that."

Now the man looked good and truly perplexed.

"Maybe I have the wrong house," Stephanie said. "I'm looking for Agnes Wharton. She's a writer."

His face brightened. "Actually, you are in the right place. Agnes is out back working in the garden. I'm her husband."

"Jedd?" she asked.

He started. Then he laughed. "Oh, I see. Good one. No, my name's Roger. Come on out this way."

No Jedd? Instead, a Roger. The facts clicked into place. Jedd had not made it back on that fateful night recorded on the last page of *Sea Comes Knocking*. Fast-forward twenty years, and Agnes was now married to a man who looked as though he might be an accountant or an insurance agent. It made her feel odd. *Of course people change in two decades, you ninny. As long as Agnes's sequel captures the drama and angst from those early Jedd years, things will turn out just fine.*

The house was sleek and modern inside, with abstract prints in neutral tones complementing soft beige walls. Elegant leather furniture and tall shelves of books adorned the living room. The kitchen featured granite countertops and a vase with three brilliant yellow sunflowers. It opened onto chic French doors that led to a tiled patio that offered cushioned chairs and a massive glass table.

Odd, so odd, so out of step with her expectations. But it was a common error, confusing an author's work on the page with their actual life. *A literary agent should know better,* she chided herself. She wondered suddenly what Ian would have made of the situation.

Roger opened the French doors and gestured. "Go just out past that shed. She's working on the pole beans today, though we've got enough beans to last us until the next millennium. I'm knee-deep in an Excel spreadsheet so I'll let you go find her by yourself."

An Excel spreadsheet. How...normal. "Right," Stephanie said faintly.

She guided Sweetness along, tugging when he wished to stop and urinate on the massive terra-cotta pots that stood sentry on either side of the patio. "Come on. You can pee on that later. Let's go see your mama."

She tugged Sweetness along a flagstone path, past a tidy painted shed with a shake roof. Beyond was a burgeoning garden, bordered by a split rail fence. Precise plots of soil ballooned with life, spilling their green entrails over onto narrow paths in between. Even with her limited sense of the natural world, Stephanie recognized eggplant, squash, and cucumbers. Some trellises struggled to hold up climbing pole beans, and others propped up blackberry bushes that bristled with fruit and thorns.

Stephanie's pulse ticked up. Agnes bent over one of the trellises. Her hair was pulled back into her trademark braid and she wore jeans and a striped T-shirt. A bandana was tucked into her back pocket.

Stephanie found herself in need of a strengthening breath. Here it was. The Moment.

Sweetness didn't seem to understand the gravity of the homecoming because he was still sniffing madly, this time nosing around some sort of squash that Stephanie had never seen before. She cleared her throat.

"Mrs. Wharton?"

Agnes jerked, whirling to face her. She blinked and squinted. "Stephanie Pink?"

"Yes, ma'am. I've come for the manuscript and..."

But Agnes's gaze was riveted on Sweetness. Stephanie stopped talking, allowing the tender reunion to unfold. Agnes's Sweetness, her baby, returned to her at long last.

Agnes finally managed speech.

"Get that awful animal away from my squash!"

~ ∽ ~

Rhett was half crazed by the time he picked up Jack and Laura from the side of the road. They'd hunkered down in the shade of a ragged pile of rocks after Jack placed a call to Rhett and explained that Stephanie had absconded with his truck.

"Dunno what happened," Jack said as he helped Rhett add some fuel to Laura's gas tank. "Seemed like she kinda went crazy."

Laura shook her head in disgust. "Well, my time here in this hole-in-the-wall has been wasted. Stephanie got to Agnes first by car thievery. Who would do that?"

As she yanked her vehicle into a precarious U-turn and headed back down the mountain, Rhett had the sense that Laura would have done exactly the same thing. Ruthless, these literary agents, and that manuscript was much more than a simple business deal to Stephanie.

Rhett and Jack continued up the mountain. As soon as they drew even with the truck parked in Agnes Wharton's driveway, Jack handed Rhett Stephanie's purse, hopped out, and made for his vehicle.

"I'm sure she will want to apologize to you and thank you again for letting her, uh, borrow your truck," Rhett called.

Jack didn't even look back. He fired up the engine and drove away before any more madness could strike.

Rhett was relieved that he saw no sign of the police car yet.

He knocked, and the door was answered by a peeved-looking man with glasses. He took in the sleek black purse in Rhett's hand.

Rhett hurried to explain. "I'm looking for a woman."

"Let me guess. The lady and her dog who arrived here earlier?"

"Yes, sir. Are they here?"

"You'll find them in the garden. You can make your way out there through the kitchen. If you'll excuse me, I need to get back to my spreadsheet." Pointing in the way they should go, he marched off into the hallway.

Rhett had been expecting more of a Grizzly Adams type, but he didn't take the time to stew on it. He hastened out through the back door and dashed toward the garden. Raised female voices and excited barking indicated he was probably too late, but he ran anyway.

He found Stephanie standing dumbfounded next to a tangle of squash plants. Agnes glared at her, snapping a pair of garden gloves in an accusatory manner.

Sweetness galloped over and gave Rhett a slobbery greeting.

Stephanie showed no surprise when both women turned to look at Rhett.

"You're not going to believe this," she said.

"I absolutely am."

Stephanie shook her head as if she hadn't heard him. "No, I mean you're really not going to believe this. Sweetness..." she looked in round-eyed disbelief at the dog.

"Isn't Sweetness," Rhett finished.

Agnes snorted. "Exactly what I've been trying to tell this woman. Sweetness is a pedigreed Samoyed. He is having his nails done right now."

"But...but back in Big Thumb, you said...you asked me to find Sweetness."

She waved a glove. "Some trucker on his way out of town saw Sweetness by the side of the road. He called the number on his tag, and my husband called me. I picked up Sweetness before I cleared the state line."

"Hold on," Stephanie said. "I thought you didn't believe in talking on the phone."

"I don't," she said, aiming a withering look at Stephanie. "Not to literary agents. I would *never* give an agent my phone number."

Stephanie gaped. "So I've been lugging this dog across three states, and he isn't even yours?"

"Correct."

"Whose is he, then?"

"How would I know the answer to that?"

In a moment of perfect timing, Roger slid open the patio door, looking even more annoyed than he had earlier. He shooed the police officer onto the patio. The officer was followed by a familiar-looking woman whom Rhett could not place at first.

"That dog is Bert," the officer said. "He belongs to Gene, who runs the Cup of Mud back in Big Thumb."

"Yeah," said Evonne, crouching down to accept an exuberant greeting from the dog. "And because you swiped Bert, my uncle wants to press charges for dognapping against both of you."

"Uncle Gene? At the diner?"

"Well," Rhett said. "That explains the spatula fetish."

Twenty-Five

I t took a lot of talking and cajoling until Evonne agreed to take possession of Bert cum Sweetness and return to Big Thumb without having Stephanie or Rhett arrested.

Agnes graciously invited Evonne and the police officer to settle on the patio while Evonne placed a called to Uncle Gene, who burst into a crying fit so loud everyone could hear his hysterics on the phone. Agnes went to the kitchen to fill a pitcher with ice water. Stephanie followed her in. Time to put on her big-girl, I'm-a-real-literary-agent-hear-me-roar pants and get the job done.

"Mrs. Wharton, I'm sorry about the mix-up, but I did follow the intent of our agreement. I hope you will allow me to take possession of the manuscript."

Agnes didn't look at her, fussing with some glasses on a tray. "About that..."

"Klein and Gregory can get you a lucrative contract with any number of publishing houses. If any other agency has agreed to represent you, we can beat their services. I promise." She stopped, abandoning her pitch. "My brother and I read *Sea Comes Knocking* cover to cover dozens of times. It touched us and inspired us to be literary agents."

Agnes stared. "Really?"

"Yes."

"You and your brother?"

She blinked back tears and nodded.

"You're in business together because of my book?"

"Ian died when he was sixteen, but he would be so thrilled, so overwhelmed to know that I am here now to represent you, and that your second book is ready to launch into the world. We spent hours imagining what happened to you and Jedd after he left on that rainy night."

Agnes chewed her lip. "I had no idea. I mean, they're just words on sheets of paper. That's all."

"Not just words. They were your life. Yours and Jedd's." Stephanie's voice broke and she hoped Agnes hadn't heard. Then again, maybe it would be okay to let some emotion in, to show Agnes how much her story had touched others.

Agnes sighed, deep and low. "In high school, I was in love with a boy named Jay Peter Simmons. He died in a motorcycle accident our senior year."

"You put flowers on his grave back in Big Thumb."

"Yes, I do that every year. That's why I was there and arranged to meet you. During our meeting, I was going to explain things. Clear the air finally. Get you people to stop hounding me."

"Explain what things?"

"My book, *Sea Comes Knocking*." She circled the rim of a water glass with her finger. "It wasn't a memoir."

"Wasn't...what?"

"It's fiction."

Fiction? Why was Agnes making no sense? "It's a memoir. It says so right on the cover," Stephanie said stupidly.

Agnes rolled her eyes. "You can't judge a book by its cover."

"Yes, you can. People do. All the time. What are you talking about? Your story about you and Jedd..."

"There is no Jedd!" Agnes snapped. "I wrote the story after Jay Peter died. On a lark I sent it to Klein and Gregory, and somehow they got the idea it was a memoir and signed me. I needed the money. I was too embarrassed to correct them."

Stephanie's brain felt flabby and slow. "But...Jedd and baby Violet? The cabin in the mountains?"

"All made up, honey," she said quietly. "It kind of snowballed."

Stephanie stood there breathing hard. Her mind whirled from the impact. *Damage control!* her mind screamed. What would Mr. Klein say? "We can tell the truth now and market it as fiction. Your writing is so lyrical, so moving, people will buy it anyway. When the second book comes out..."

"There is no second book," Agnes said, pulling a box from the drawer. "I just told you that because you all kept sending me letters and pestering me about it. Then in Big Thumb I needed you to find my dog, so I let the charade continue." She sighed. "I'm really not a very nice person." She thrust the box at Stephanie.

Stephanie looked inside at the sheaf of papers, all blank pages.

"There is no second book?"

"No. I'm not a writer. I never wanted to be. *Sea Comes Knocking* was just a way for me to work through my grief when Jay Peter died. I never intended to write anything else, and I never will. The book earns enough to keep me living comfortably, and that's sufficient."

"But my brother and I..."

Her face softened. "I didn't know people would be so...invested. I never meant to trick anyone or to lie. It's just made up, words on pages. I'm sorry if I hurt you." She cocked her head. "I didn't realize how powerful a story could be until just this moment."

A memoir that wasn't, the book that launched her dream, Ian's dream. Made up. She looked up to see Rhett watching from the doorway, his face grave.

They stood staring at each other until Rhett put his hand on her shoulder. The gesture broke the spell.

And then, somehow, the strange party was ushered out of Agnes Wharton's house. The police officer got behind the wheel of his car, and Evonne shook hands with Stephanie and Rhett.

"I am very sorry for upsetting Uncle Gene," Stephanie managed. "I'm going to apologize to him personally before I fly back to New York."

Evonne laughed. "That won't be necessary. This is going to make a great story when I write it up." She turned to Rhett. "I'll be calling you for some quotes, okay?"

Rhett's eyes narrowed.

"It's the least you can do after the trouble you've caused," Evonne said firmly.

Rhett grumbled something.

A great story. For sure. It had all the components save one...a happy ending. Stephanie knelt to say goodbye to Sweetness.

"I'm going to miss you, Sweetness." Tears unleashed themselves, hot and unexpected. The dog licked her face, unconcerned at the mess she'd made of her entire adult life. Sweetness flapped his ears and allowed her to caress the satiny spot behind each one. No book, no dream, no plan, no Sweetness.

"And I even managed to become a dognapper along the way," she whispered, her cheek against his bony head. "I'm sorry for taking you away from your family. You must have missed them so much."

Sweetness went still. His tongue stopped its relentless licking, and he simply stood silent in her arms, accepting the love she gave and holding back none of his own.

Rhett knelt next to her to add his own canine caresses. "You're a good boy, Sweetness. You take care of Uncle Gene, okay?" He gave the dog his chewed spatula, and they watched as Evonne and the police officer got him settled and then drove away.

Stephanie shaded her eyes against the brilliant sunlight. The door of 1 Eagle Cliff Road was shut firmly behind her. She was un-tethered once again, like the moment the bus had deposited her in Big Thumb and driven away with all her earthly possessions, like the moment they'd told her Ian was dead.

"Can I give you a ride someplace, Stephanie?" Rhett said. "Maybe we could head back to Dappled Acres."

Why, exactly? What was waiting there for Stephanie Pink? She should go home. But her New York apartment seemed as though it might be in a different universe, a moon around a planet that was caving in on itself, sending everything skittering out of orbit. Her life plan, the destiny she'd written for herself, was based on a flimsy fiction, a made-up story, a cosmic mistake. How perfectly ludicrous.

How perfectly Stephanie.

∞

Rhett moved next to her and reached out his hand, stopping before he made contact. Her face was so rigid and tense, he worried that the slightest touch might just shatter her into jagged pieces. She stood ramrod straight. "It's getting late and you must be hungry." It was lame, but he wasn't sure what else to offer. "It's…are we… do you want to talk about it?" He was fairly certain that was what a sensitive person would say.

She bit her lip and looked at him. "Rhett, I've spent years and years chasing a box full of blank paper."

He didn't answer.

"Well? What do you have to say about that?"

"I'm trying to think. I don't want to be an insensitive blubber head, and this off-the-cuff stuff doesn't usually show me in my best light."

She let out a harsh laugh. "It's not like you could make the situation any worse. Just don't tell me this is God's plan for me, okay?"

The anguish in her eyes made him want to gather her close.

"I'm sorry things didn't turn out. I've experienced that feeling often recently."

"But you knew all along that my plans were misguided."

He winced as he recalled their conversation in the trailer, his typically brash words. *"And it doesn't have to be your life's work to preserve a plan your brother cooked up when you were teens, either. You aren't frozen there, in that time, just because he died then."*

He blew out a breath. "For some reason, it's always easier for me to see the flaw in someone else's plan than in my own."

"You were right. You should be glad."

"But I'm not. You're hurting, and I'm sorry for it."

She looked at her shoes, scuffing one toe in the dirt. "Why did you come up here?"

"Well, I didn't want you to get arrested, for one thing."

"And the other thing?"

He shifted, rubbed a hand over his stubbled chin. "This might not be the time."

"It's the perfect time."

"No, no. I'm pretty sure it's not. I have terrible timing with women. Just ask my sister. Karen would say this is absolutely not an appropriate time."

"Rhett, stop babbling and tell me." She eyed him. "You look... different. Relaxed and...taller."

He chuckled. "I think that's because a huge weight is off my shoulders."

She raised an eyebrow.

He cleared his throat. "I...I've decided to stick around with Karen and help her get the orchard going again."

She gaped. "Why?"

"Because you were right."

"I was? About what?"

He kicked at a rock on the ground. "I finally saw what was alive in the orchard, in my life, and I realized I've been trying to make God fit into my plans instead of the other way around."

He saw that his words spurred a storm of feelings. He tried to imagine what she was thinking. Why should he stand there and spout off hard-won wisdom about God when her life had just fallen apart? He'd said it all wrong. Again.

"Well, good for you."

"Stephanie, I—"

"No, really. I'm thrilled that you're embracing God's plans for you. Personally, I don't want Him mucking around in mine. Recently I've sort of tried to, you know, open my mind on account of you and all this and Mrs. Granato."

He had no idea who Mrs. Granato was.

"But you know what?" Her eyes shone with tears. "That was a mistake. I'm looking around here, and I don't see hope and a future. I have a dead brother and a smashed wedding cake, and my big shot at the career I've planned for just got blown to smithereens. I don't want God interfering."

"I think maybe love looks a lot like interference sometimes," he said quietly.

She shook her head so hard the hair whipped her cheeks. "God took my brother, and just now He took away my dream. I don't like the plans He has for me, Rhett. He doesn't love me."

"Yes, He does." Rhett caught up her hands and then locked eyes with her. "And so do I."

He'd said it. Now he watched, breath stilled, as his future unfolded before him.

Twenty-Six

Stephanie's eyes widened, and her lush fringe of lashes sparkled with tears that had not yet fallen. Those eyes were the loveliest thing Rhett had ever seen. He discovered that he'd forgotten to breathe.

"You love me?" she whispered.

His insides clenched, and he went light-headed. He could deny it, say it was love in a friendly, people-who-shared-a-ludicrous-journey kind of way. Instead, he let himself believe the truth that was anchored deep down in his bones and braided around the cords of his heart. He nodded slowly, ready to utter the bravest words he'd ever spoken. "Yes, Stephanie Pink. I love you."

He took her hand and leaned in, brushing his lips over her cheek and finally finding her mouth. He kissed her, slow and sweet. Ribbons of joy welled up, leaving him no doubt that Stephanie was the woman God made for Rhett Hastings to love. He'd had to turn his life upside down and shake out the pockets and climb aboard an old trailer with a couple of nutty dogs to do it. He'd had to face his darkest sin and ask humbly for forgiveness. Such a long and convoluted journey, but worth every moment.

When he lifted his head, she looked at him in awe. "Why? Why do you love me?"

He struggled to make his mouth explain the fullness of his heart. "Because you are a dreamer. You see promise in wrecked things." He swallowed. "You saw the promise in me."

"That doesn't make me lovable."

"There are many more reasons, Stephanie. You're smart and funny."

She shook her head. "Plenty of people are like that. The Chain Gang's full of women of that ilk."

"You use words like 'ilk,' you say kind things, and you dream about opening a bookstore that will delight people of all ages."

Her head fell. "Stupid dream."

He crooked a finger under her chin and lifted it until he could once again face those shimmering eyes. "It's a Stephanie Pink dream, and that makes it perfect."

She stared at him, her brows drawn.

He trailed a finger across her cheek. "And you know how to make exotic delicacies out of bologna and white bread."

She did not smile. Dread burgeoned inside him, but he kept on.

One of his fingers caressed a silken strand of her hair. "And you are a tender soul in a calloused world, a person who makes others shine brighter because they are near you."

Stephanie sighed. "Rhett, you're a good man, and I think...that I love you too."

His heart soared. *Love you too.* "Then you'll stay here?"

She shook her head. "No."

No. It could not be no. "If it's because of your job..."

She put her hands on his shoulders until he stopped talking. "Rhett, I'm a dreamer without a dream right now. I can't make plans with you because then I'd be following your plans instead of mine. But I'm happy." Her fingers drifted down his arms and she squeezed his hands. "I'm really happy that you've found your way."

"His way."

She let go, a flicker of anger tightening her mouth. "I'm not ready to go His way. Maybe I never will be."

"You don't have to be ready right now," he said, desperate to convince her. "I wasn't for a very long time. God's patient, that one I'm sure of."

She gave him a sad smile. "I'll never forget you, Rhett, and I hope you and Karen will love your new lives. It's time for me to go find mine."

He couldn't bear it. He pulled her to him and kissed her again. She kissed him back, and then she cupped a hand to his cheek with a soft sigh. "Thank you for everything."

Thank you. And goodbye. He was numb.

"If it isn't too much to ask, would you take me to the nearest bus station? I need to stop in Big Thumb and apologize before I fly back to New York."

Practical. Tie up all the loose ends. His heart throbbed with agony. What could he say? How could he make her understand? If he was Agnes Wharton, he could pour his love and tenderness into words so eloquent she would never leave him. He would weave her into his story with an unforgettable plot twist. But he had no clever words, no exquisite turn of phrase to prove to her that his love ran deeper than her hurt, her doubt. He saw the certainty in her eyes, the finality of her decision.

"Yes," he said faintly. He went to the truck and opened the passenger door for her.

The front seat seemed cavernous without Sweetness sprawled between them. Stephanie stared out the window as Rhett drove the truck down the mountain, leaving Agnes and her box of empty pages behind.

∽

The apology session started with Uncle Gene waving a ladle and rattling off angry phrases in Portuguese while Sweetness-Bert licked Stephanie on every square inch he could access. It ended with a gracious acceptance and a feast of Bert's famous corned beef and egg scramble, along with an invitation to sleep in a tiny guest room/office above the diner.

The next morning after another of Uncle Gene's specials, she found herself filled to bursting, sitting on a bench that passed for the Big Thumb bus stop. Sweetness snored at her feet, also filled with scrambled eggs. Uncle Gene peeked out the window of the Cup of Mud every so often, probably to make sure Stephanie had no intention of committing another dog abduction. She was, after all, from New York City.

How odd she felt, sitting on this little bench, staring at the quiet, tree-lined street without a single car to be seen. The New York City bustle seemed such a distant memory, though she would be back there in the wee hours that very day.

Back there. Briefing Mr. Klein about the whole debacle, which was surely not her fault. There simply was no book, no story, but there would be other authors to pursue, and she knew eventually she would see her name on that office window. Klein, Gregory, and Pink.

She caught her reflection in the empty store window. Was she that small? That ordinary? A woman sitting with a dog at a bus stop in a rural nowhere. Her plans with Ian had made her feel removed from such an ordinary life. They had been her close companion for all the years since his death. She'd been pursuing a higher purpose, an uncommon calling, she'd believed.

Funny. How she'd give up all her glamorous notions and visions of success just to have her brother sitting next to her on that ordinary bench in that nondescript town, a million miles away from New York City.

"But Ian's not here," she muttered savagely, earning a poke from Sweetness. "You took him away, God." Her eyes filled. "You hurt me."

The sun warmed her face, and her fingers found the little book Mrs. Granato had given her a lifetime ago upon her arrival in Big Thumb.

I know the plans I have for you...

Would it have hurt so much, God, to let me see my plans through? To become that agent for Ian?

For Ian. Her body went hot, then cold.

Rhett had been right. She'd borrowed her brother's dream. She'd picked it up like a trailing leash and let it run with her through the days and years of her life.

So what? So what if I did confuse Ian's dreams with mine? There was no harm in it. She'd been a great literary assistant.

And Rhett had been a massively successful movie mogul.

But they'd both been hanging on to that leash, sprinting to catch up with a plan that was of their own making. Not God's.

Not God's.

Sweetness rolled on top of her feet then, wriggling against her thrift store shoes to massage his back. His paws bicycled through the air. She laughed out loud, once again catching sight of herself in the window glass.

Where did that smile on her face come from? Ian was gone and her blockbuster novel had vanished, but her mind was filled with the thought of all the things she'd collected on her crazed coastal trailer trip.

A lifelong friend in Karen.

A standing invitation to visit Big Thumb.

The affection of an ancient dog saved by another dog who took blessings as he found them.

Her seatmate on the bus.

And the love of a man, a very good man, an arrogant yet humble man, who had given her a new appreciation for French onion soup.

She laughed again, reaching down to scratch Sweetness behind the ears.

∽

Rhett got the e-mail just before Thanksgiving. It arrived via the Dappled Acres website he'd set up. No name attached. *That's odd,* he thought. Why couldn't this guy have phoned or texted to arrange for a supply of Dappled Acres apples to be resold at his store? But then Rhett's job was to cater to buyers of any kind who would market the apples, jellies, pies, and cakes that Karen and her helpers produced.

He'd only made it through a few weeks as a farmhand before being shooed out of the day-to-day operations. Karen said he was far too bossy and impatient to work with others. She was right, of course, and he enjoyed the travel, the excitement of landing a deal, the joy of flying over the lush fall foliage of fall. Sometimes he'd bring Panny along when she could be convinced to leave Bunny. She'd grown stronger, and his clients didn't seem to mind the tiny elderly dog tucked into his jacket.

He'd bought a well-appointed cabin in Oregon because there was room for a landing strip. Before he'd even unpacked, he'd made arrangements to be reunited with his beloved aircraft. Thanks to his plane, he had easy access to Dappled Acres and enough distance to give Karen some breathing room. The hulk of a trailer remained on the Dapple Acres property even after she'd had the house restored to a livable condition so he could sleep over during his frequent visits. The rest of the time, he puttered around his cabin. He'd worried he'd hate the quiet, but he found that he enjoyed it, and the multitude of home and business projects kept his mind off of Stephanie. Mostly.

He often found himself, screwdriver in hand, staring into space trying to imagine what she was doing, picturing the mischievous glint in her eyes, her laugh—much louder than it should be for one so small—and the earnest lilt in her voice when she'd said, "I think... that I love you too."

He held on to those words on long nights when he couldn't sleep. During days when he missed her so badly that he drove for miles with no particular destination in mind, stopping in everywhere he saw a movie theater to take in a show, wishing she was sitting next to him. Daily he restrained himself from checking her agency website. That would accomplish nothing but tear open the wound in his heart. Again.

Don still called occasionally for advice, which Rhett was happy to give. Don was morphing into a top-notch CEO, and Rhett was proud to know his company was still growing and thriving. Don inked multimillion-dollar contracts, while Rhett was thrilled to score much smaller deals for apples and baked goods.

He secured the plane, rented a car, and began the drive to Big Thumb, arriving at the address he'd been given.

Right next door to the Cup of Mud. It must be a mistake. There was nothing at that location but an empty storefront. He got out and double-checked the e-mail.

Sighing, he figured he might as well go visit Sweetness and enjoy a cup of coffee and a bowl of navy bean soup to ward off the chill when the door of the empty storefront opened and Sweetness barreled out.

Rhett bent to greet him and laughed as he endured the slurping tongue. "What are you doing in there, boy?"

"He's helping me." Stephanie stepped out, wearing jeans and a long-sleeved T-shirt, her hair pulled back into a ponytail, a streak of dust on her cheek, looking more beautiful than he had remembered.

∽

Rhett was so shocked to see her he lost his balance and sat hard on the ground. Sweetness got in some extra licks while Rhett struggled to his feet, standing so fast he went dizzy.

"Stephanie?"

She smiled. "It's good to see you, Rhett."

"You...what are you doing here? Did you send me the e-mail?"

"Yes. I wanted to invite you to my soft opening. We're going to have a big event later, of course. I thought we might need some pie for that. And some cider. Books go well with cider." Then she walked back into the store, leaving him to gape.

Sweetness jogged across the threshold, turning to give him a look that said, "*Well, are you just going to stand there like a clueless human?*" Rhett closed his mouth and, heart pounding, went inside.

The place was a wreck, his gut told him. But his heart did not seem to record anything but the fact that Stephanie Pink stood in the center of the marred wood floor, smiling. At him.

A gray cat with part of an ear missing twined around Rhett's ankles.

"That's Biscuit. Sweetness lugged her in here last week. I think she's mine now. Very sweet, but I told her no more bringing me dead birds as presents." She shuddered. "Gross."

"Stephanie," he finally managed. "What...what is all this?"

"It's my bookstore." Her eyes narrowed. "Now, I know what you're thinking. It's a wreck, but look at it this way." She went to him and crooked her arm through his. "Over there," she said, pointing to a dingy corner stacked with broken pallets, "that's the kids' corner. There will be beanbag chairs. And music. And pretend trees—kind of a forest theme."

He let himself be towed along. "And here is the grown-up reading area, which will house excellent books that real people want to read and some of the fancier, hoity-toity variety that most people don't want to read. And there will be comfy chairs and a table for those who want to grab coffee and knit while they talk about books.

The Chain Gang, by the way, is going to fly out for the grand opening. They promised."

She smiled.

He gaped. "Stephanie...you're opening a bookstore?"

She nodded.

"In Big Thumb?"

She nodded again.

"You're not going to be a literary agent? But it was your dream."

She released him and sat down on an overturned bucket. "No, it was my brother's dream, just like you said. God has another plan for me. Once I stopped chasing after the leash, it became clear to me."

"What leash?"

"Not important," she said, her chin on her hands. "Rhett, it's focus time now, so listen up because I'm only going to have the courage to say this once. You are the bravest man I know, and you helped me to be brave. I'm ready to run after another dream, my dream, the one God meant for me to have."

He couldn' answer.

"So I'm staying," she said. "Here. Near Sweetness and not so far from Dappled Acres...and sharing a coast with you."

"Me?" He hardly dared breathe.

She looked at her toes, suddenly shy. "I love you. You're an odd mix-up of things. You're brave and humble and arrogant and snobby and sweet and ferocious and gentle...and I love you. I want us to grow a life together." She peeked at him out of the corner of her eye. "I mean, if you're still interested."

He was frozen to the spot.

"Because, full disclosure, I still like bologna and cheese and cheap novels and microwave popcorn."

He was electrified, afraid to believe his ears.

"You...really are...and we're..."

She laughed. "Rhett Hastings, I believe you're speechless."

And he was, completely unable to render a coherent sentence except for four words. "I love you, Stephanie."

He took her hands, tugged her into his arms, and swung her in a circle, which made Sweetness bark and Biscuit take cover.

She threw her arms around him, laughing. "I know you can fly anywhere, but I was thinking maybe we can find some middle ground between Big Thumb and your place in Oregon. I mean, if you didn't mind relocating. There's plenty of land here if you wanted to put in a landing strip."

"For you, I'd live anywhere."

She laughed some more and he kissed her, and then he kissed her again. When they were both out of breath, he put her down.

"You know, if you hadn't started chasing that crazy dog past my trailer, we never would have met," he told her, gazing into the eyes he'd called up in his memory for four long months.

"I'm going to buy Sweetness a new spatula to thank him."

He stroked her hair as he felt the joy of her arms around his waist. "Oh, somehow I think he knows he's a one-of-a-kind dog."

Sweetness looked from Rhett to Stephanie and leaped into the air, his ears flapping and jowls wobbling. His bark echoed through the ruined storefront, filling the space with his own particular kind of joy.

About the Author

Dana Mentink lives in California, where the weather is golden and the cheese is divine. Dana is a two-time American Christian Fiction Writers Book of the Year winner for romantic suspense and a Holt Medallion Merit award recipient. Her suspense novel, *Betrayal in the Badlands*, earned a Romantic Times Reviewer's Choice Award.

Besides writing, Dana busies herself teaching third grade. Mostly, she loves to be home with her husband, two daughters, a hyperactive mutt, a chubby box turtle, and a feisty parakeet.

Visit her on the web at www.danamentink.com.

DANA MENTINK

"I've asked everyone from the shortstop to the hot dog vendors, and no one wants a thirteen-year-old mutt."

Pro baseball pitcher Cal Crawford is not a dog guy. When he inherits his deceased mother's elderly dog, Tippy, he's quick to call on a pet-sitting service.

Gina isn't thrilled to be a dog sitter when her aspirations lie in the classroom. Furthermore, she can't abide the unfriendly Cal, a man with all the charm of a wet towel. But with no other prospects and a deep love for all things canine, she takes the job caring for Tippy.

As Gina travels through Cal's world with Tippy in tow, she begins to see Cal in a different light. Gina longs to show Cal the God-given blessings in his life that have nothing to do with baseball or fame. This pro athlete, along with an out-of-work teacher and an overweight, geriatric dog, is about to get a lesson in love...Tippy-style.

The author is committed to donating a portion
of the proceeds toward senior dog rescue.

Want another entertaining, romantic, and tail-wagging story
involving hapless humans and an adorable dog?

Don't Miss

Paws for Love

Coming Soon to Your Favorite Retailer

To learn more about Harvest House books and
to read sample chapters, visit our website:

www.harvesthousepublishers.com

HARVEST HOUSE PUBLISHERS
EUGENE, OREGON